Sweet Revenge

Stephanie reached into the bag and grabbed one of the hideous pink shower caps. She held it out to Rene.

Rene stared at the cap. Her mouth dropped open in horror. "I'm not wearing that—that *thing*," she sputtered.

"You'd better wear it, Rene," Darcy told her. "Everyone at the pool knows about our big bet. If you don't wear the cap, you'll really look like a bad sport."

"Yeah. Everyone will say you're chicken," Kayla added.

Rene glared at all of them. She snatched the cap from Stephanie's hand and pulled it over her blond ponytail. She handed caps to Alyssa, Mary, and Julie—the other members of the swim team. They pulled them on. The enormous caps stuck out over their ears and flopped onto their foreheads. They all looked ridiculous.

Darcy snickered. Allie and Kayla held their hands over their mouths, covering giggles. Anna laughed out loud.

Stephanie grinned. It felt great to see the Flamingoes humiliated for once!

"All right, Stephanie—you win this one," Rene declared. "But you won't win what really matters." Her blue eyes narrowed to a squint. "You'll never win Rick!"

FULL HOUSE™: Stephanie novels

Phone Call from a Flamingo
The Boy-Oh-Boy Next Door
Twin Troubles
Hip Hop Till You Drop
Here Comes the Brand-New Me
The Secret's Out
Daddy's Not-So-Little Girl
P.S. Friends Forever
Getting Even with the Flamingoes
The Dude of My Dreams
Back-to-School Cool
Picture Me Famous
Two-for-One Christmas Fun
The Big Fix-up Mix-up
Ten Ways to Wreck a Date
Wish Upon a VCR
Doubles or Nothing
Sugar and Spice Advice
Never Trust a Flamingo
The Truth About Boys
Crazy About the Future

Club Stephanie:

#1 Sun, Fun, and Flamingoes
#2 Fireworks and Flamingoes
#3 Flamingo Revenge

Available from MINSTREL Books

FULL HOUSE™

Club Stephanie

Flamingo Revenge

**Based on the hit Warner Bros.
TV series**

Janet Quin-Harkin

A Parachute Press Book

READING

A
MINSTREL®
BOOK

Published by POCKET BOOKS
New York   London   Toronto   Sydney   Tokyo   Singapore

A MINSTREL PAPERBACK *Original*

 A Minstrel Book published by
POCKET BOOKS, a division of Simon & Schuster Inc.
1230 Avenue of the Americas, New York, NY 10020

A PARACHUTE PRESS BOOK

 Copyright © and ™ 1997 by Warner Bros.

FULL HOUSE, characters, names and all related indicia are trademarks of Warner Bros. © 1997.

ISBN: 0-671-00828-5

First Minstrel Books printing August 1997

10 9 8 7 6 5 4 3 2 1

A MINSTREL BOOK and colophon are registered trademarks of Simon & Schuster Inc.

Cover photo by Schultz Photography

Printed in the U.S.A.

Flamingo Revenge

CHAPTER
1

◆ ◢ ◣ ◆

Dear Rick:
  I'm breaking up with you because you're a
terrible kisser.
  Sorry,
  Stephanie

"Read this!" Stephanie Tanner's blue eyes blazed
with anger. She tossed her head, flinging her long
blond hair over one shoulder.

She waved the letter in front of her best friend
Allie Taylor's face. "Can you believe it?" Stephanie
fumed. "Those rotten Flamingoes switched *my* letter with *this* one!"

Allie grabbed the note and read it. She gasped
in horror. "Oh, no! No wonder Rick won't talk to

you!'' she exclaimed. "This note is awful! He must have been so humiliated!"

Boom! Boom!

Red, white, and blue fireworks exploded in the sky overhead. It was the Fourth of July. Stephanie, Allie, and all of their friends were gathered at the local community center for a big picnic celebration. The day had been crammed with activities, ending with the fireworks that filled the sky.

Stephanie had been so excited about the picnic. Now all she could think about was Rick and how furious—and hurt—he must be.

Rick Summers was sixteen and an assistant lifeguard at the pool. He was also cute, and fun, and totally cool.

At first, Stephanie could hardly believe that he liked her as much as she liked him. But it was true. Stephanie was having the best summer of her life—until the Flamingoes stepped in.

"I hate those Flamingoes!" Allie exclaimed.

Allie was usually quiet and shy. But right now she scowled with anger. She looked ready to take on the Flamingoes all by herself.

The Flamingoes were a group of snobby girls. They always hung out together. They always wore bright pink. And they were always super-mean to Stephanie and her friends. Worst of all, Rene Salter, the head Flamingo, was jealous of Stephanie. She had been trying to break up Rick and Stephanie all summer.

Rene liked Rick, too. And one awful night, Stephanie caught Rene kissing Rick!

After that, Stephanie tried to forget about Rick. But no matter how hard she tried, she couldn't stop thinking about him. Then she learned the truth. Rene had tricked Rick into kissing her!

Stephanie wanted to let Rick know how much she still cared for him. *Really* cared for him. So she wrote him a letter. She remembered every word:

. . . You may not believe this, but I like you more than I ever liked any boy before.

If you like me, even a little, couldn't we start over again? What do you say?

She left the note in his backpack. Then she waited and waited, but Rick never answered. Instead he avoided Stephanie. He wouldn't return her phone calls. And worst of all, he started hanging out with Rene and the Flamingoes. And now she knew why!

"Rick never even saw the letter I wrote him!" Stephanie exclaimed in disbelief. "He thinks I said he's a terrible kisser. What will I do, Allie?" Stephanie bit her lip. "Rick must really, really hate me!"

"This is the worst thing those Flamingoes have ever done," Allie declared.

"Well, Rene's not getting away with this!" Stephanie turned and rushed away.

"Wait, Steph! Where are you going?" Allie called.

"To find Rene—and tell her that I know what she did!" Stephanie replied. Allie raced after her.

The community center was jam-packed. The pool was in the middle of the center. It was a popular hangout for the teens in the neighborhood. And little kids came every day to Club Stephanie—the day camp run by Stephanie and her friends. But today everyone's families and friends had crammed onto the center's lawn for the big picnic celebration. Stephanie and Allie had to fight their way through the crowd.

"Stephanie! Allie! Over here!" Darcy Taylor, Stephanie's other best friend, jumped to her feet. Her black hair flew wildly around her face.

Darcy grinned, but her grin faded when she saw the expression on Stephanie's face. "What's wrong? What happened?" she demanded.

Stephanie, Allie, and Darcy were longtime best friends. Stephanie always counted on Allie for good advice and on Darcy for always speaking her mind.

4

"I'll tell you what happened. This!" Stephanie thrust the crumpled note at Darcy.

Anna Rice and Kayla Norris scrambled to their feet to read the note over Darcy's shoulder. Anna and Kayla had volunteered to be counselors for Club Stephanie earlier that summer. In only a few weeks, Anna and Kayla had become much more than co-counselors—they were good friends, too. Stephanie, Darcy, and Allie felt as if they had known the two new girls forever.

"Is this some kind of joke?" Anna exploded. She shook her head so hard that her bead earrings jingled together. Anna taught arts and crafts at Club Stephanie. She loved making her own clothing and jewelry. She had her own unique sense of style. And her own opinions—about everything.

"It's a pretty bad joke," Kayla added.

"Who do you think gave Rick the note, Steph?" Anna asked.

Stephanie's gaze shifted across the pool area. A huge pink umbrella stood out against the night sky. The umbrella was decorated with little flamingoes and long, pink fringe. The Flamingoes were grouped under the umbrella, talking and laughing with a crowd of boys.

Stephanie's eyes narrowed. "I don't know, exactly. Alyssa Norman was on lifeguard duty when

I left my letter in Rick's backpack. Maybe she took it out and put the phony note in."

Alyssa was Rene's sidekick. She combed her ash blond hair in exactly the same style as Rene's. And she said—and did—anything Rene told her to do.

"It might have been Alyssa," Stephanie went on. "But the rest of the Flamingoes were around, too. Rene, Julie, and Mary were having swimming practice. The others were watching."

"Any one of them could have taken your note and switched it for this one," Darcy said. "But I bet it was Rene."

"Sure, it was," Allie added. "Rene would do anything to get Rick away from you. She can't stand it that he likes you, Steph."

"You mean, he *did* like me," Stephanie corrected. "Not anymore. It makes me so mad just thinking about it!"

Darcy put an arm around Stephanie's shoulders. "Don't worry, Steph. Just tell Rick that the note he read was a fake."

"How can I do that?" Stephanie asked. "Rick isn't speaking to me."

"We have to make those Flamingoes admit what they did," Anna declared. "We'll make them tell Rick the truth!"

"That's exactly what I was thinking," Stephanie told her. She marched across the pool area toward the Flamingoes' umbrella. Cynthia Hanson, a tall blond girl, saw her coming. Cynthia poked Mary Kelly. Mary squinted at Stephanie with her dark eyes. She ran a hand nervously over her short dark hair, then leaned over and nudged Rene.

Rene was busy combing her long blond hair. It hung over her face, covering her blue eyes. Rene tossed back her hair and shot Mary an impatient look. Then she noticed Stephanie striding toward her.

"Stephanie!" Rene flashed her a fake smile. "I never did say congratulations on your win today."

The Flamingoes had lost a swimming relay race to Club Stephanie that afternoon. As the losers, the Flamingoes had to wear pink shower caps to the pool—for an entire day!

"I didn't come for that," Stephanie replied.

"Well, if you came to gloat about winning, just save your breath," Rene snapped back.

"Yeah, we don't have to start wearing those dumb caps until tomorrow," Alyssa added.

"Be quiet, Alyssa," Rene murmured.

Alyssa flushed red. "Well, I only meant that—"

"You can save *your* breath, Alyssa," Stephanie said, cutting her off. "I don't care about the race right now." She waved the letter in Alyssa's face. "What do you know about *this?*"

Alyssa glanced briefly at the note. "Well, the

handwriting is terrible," she said. "It looks like a second-grader wrote it."

"Actually one of *you* wrote it," Stephanie said.

"One of us?" Alyssa opened her blue eyes wide in surprise.

"What are you talking about?" Rene snorted. "No Flamingo wrote this note! It's not even written in pink ink." She grinned. The other Flamingoes laughed.

Stephanie glanced sharply at Rene, Mary, and Alyssa. Then she turned and looked at the others: Julie Chu, Tiffany Schroeder, Darah Judson, Tina Brewer, and Dominique Dobson.

"*One* of you wrote this letter and signed my name to it," Stephanie told them. "I'll prove it!"

"Go ahead and try," Rene said in a cool voice.

"Yeah. Even if one of us *did* write the note, you can't prove a thing," Cynthia said.

"But I *can* prove that Alyssa had the best chance to take the note," Stephanie said. "Alyssa came on lifeguard duty to replace Rick that day. He felt sick and went home really early, remember?"

Alyssa shrugged. "I don't remember anything. But I—"

Rene shot Alyssa a look that said "be quiet," and Alyssa stopped talking.

"One of you switched that note," Stephanie burst out. "Just admit it!"

"I'm so sorry, Stephanie," Rene said. "But we can't help you right now. We're too busy," she added with a sly smile. "We're planning where to meet the guys when the fireworks are over. We're having a little celebration of our own with some of the lifeguards. Including Rick. Did you want me to give him any message?"

Stephanie felt her cheeks burn. "You can tell Rick that I wouldn't write—" she began.

"Forget it, Steph," Allie interrupted. "Let's just go," she added. "You know they'll never admit anything." She pulled Stephanie away.

"It doesn't matter if they admit it or not," Darcy said loudly as they walked away. "We know what they did!"

Stephanie let Allie and Darcy walk her back to their picnic blanket. Anna and Kayla glanced up.

"What happened?" Kayla asked. "Did they agree to tell Rick the truth?"

"You can forget that idea," Allie murmured.

"Wow, Steph, I'm sorry," Kayla said. Anna gave her a look of sympathy.

"Switching those notes was their meanest, dirtiest trick ever," Darcy declared. "We have to get even, if it takes the rest of this summer! Right, Steph?"

"Right," Stephanie replied. "We'll teach those Flamingoes a lesson that they'll never forget.

But what? she wondered.

CHAPTER
2

♦ ◄ ♦ ♦

"Hey, Steph and Allie—over here!" Darcy waved her graceful arms.

Stephanie saw Darcy, Kayla, and Anna sitting on lounge chairs on the sunniest side of the pool. Darcy and Kayla wore tank suits. Stephanie grinned at Anna's outfit: a long Indian-print skirt and a bright purple tank top. Anna liked looking at the water, but she didn't like swimming in it.

Stephanie and Allie hurried over. "Thanks for saving us chairs, you guys," Stephanie told them.

"It was easy," Kayla said. "This place is practically empty."

Stephanie glanced quickly around. It was early Sunday morning, and the pool wasn't crowded yet. Usually that was Stephanie's favorite time of all.

She and her friends could grab the best chairs and talk without worrying about the Flamingoes. The Flamingoes always slept late on Sundays. They also liked to make a late appearance, strolling in when the place was packed so they could show off.

"Isn't it great—no little kids around!" Anna smiled. "Don't get me wrong—I love our campers. But it's nice not to worry about how to keep a bunch of four-year-olds busy."

Club Stephanie ran five mornings a week. The campers appeared each day at nine o'clock. For the next four hours, Stephanie and her friends taught them songs, helped them do arts and crafts, ran races, and splashed with them in the pool. It was fun, but it was also hard work.

Still, Stephanie and the others loved running Club Stephanie. The campers had a blast, and the parents were grateful to have such a cool program for their kids.

"Uh, yeah, camp is great," Stephanie said. She was barely paying attention. She scanned the pool area. But there was no sign of Rick.

I have to see him today, she thought. *I have to tell him that the note he read last night was a fake!*

"And a couple of Martians just landed in the pool," Allie said.

"Great," Stephanie replied.

11

Anna rolled her eyes. "Stephanie, you aren't listening at all!"

"Sorry, Anna," Stephanie said. "It's just that I was hoping Rick would be here."

"You still haven't spoken to him?" Kayla looked shocked.

Stephanie shook her head. "I called his grandmother's house when I got home last night. I woke her up, and she said Rick wasn't home yet."

Rick and his little brother, Austin, were staying with their grandmother for the summer. Their mother was an actress. She performed in plays in a lot of different cities during the summer.

"Those Flamingoes!" Allie shook her head in disbelief. "They really *did* go out after the picnic. Talk about a nonstop party!"

"Maybe the Flamingoes are holding him captive—so you can't ever talk to him!" Anna laughed, but her smile faded when she saw the look on Stephanie's face. "Sorry, Steph. I was just trying to cheer you up."

"It's okay," Stephanie told her. "I wish I *could* cheer up. I don't even blame Rick for hanging out with the Flamingoes last night. After all, he still doesn't know the truth."

"You should call him right now," Kayla declared.

"I already tried calling his house a few times

this morning," Stephanie said. "There wasn't any answer."

"Well, you'll try again later," Darcy said. "At least you'll feel better if you do *something*."

"And I bet he'll be home soon," Kayla added. "Or he might show up at the pool. Then you can explain everything."

"I hope so," Stephanie replied. "I want him to know that I would never write a mean letter like that."

"Let's talk about something more upbeat," Kayla said. "How about our revenge on the Flamingoes?" She chuckled. "They have to wear their shower caps today, remember?"

Stephanie chuckled, too. "How could we forget?" She opened her backpack and pulled out a plastic shopping bag. "Look!" She held the bag open so everyone could see.

It was filled with hideous pink shower caps.

"Allie and I bought the biggest, ugliest ones we could find," Stephanie said.

"Wow! They are so gross!" Darcy squealed. "My great-grandmother has one like that!"

"I can't wait to see Rene and Alyssa in these." Anna grinned. "I bet they'll never want to wear pink again!"

Stephanie shoved the bagful of caps under her lounge chair. She lay back and began to spread sunblock on her arms and legs. "Yup, this is more like it," she said. "A nice, peaceful morning. Waiting for the Flamingoes to show up—and be positively humiliated!"

"Uh, don't look now," Allie said, giving Stephanie a nudge. "But I don't think it's going to stay very peaceful around here."

Stephanie glanced at the pool entrance. Her little sister, Michelle, pushed her way through the turnstile. Stephanie's big sister, D.J., followed her.

Stephanie's aunt Becky was right behind them. One of her five-year-old twins perched on her shoulder. D.J. led the other twin by the hand. From so far away, Stephanie couldn't tell which twin was Nicky and which was Alex!

Stephanie grinned when she saw her family. A lot of people shared the Tanner house. Besides Michelle, D.J., Becky, and the twins, there was Stephanie's dad, Danny Tanner. And the twins' uncle, Jesse Katsopoulis. Jesse was married to Aunt Becky. And Becky and Danny were co-hosts of *Wake Up, San Francisco*, a popular local TV show. And Joey Gladstone, Danny's former college roommate, had an apartment in the basement.

Things sometimes got crazy with so many people around. That was one reason Stephanie loved hanging out at the pool—with only her friends.

"You're right, Allie." Stephanie grinned. "It's not going to be very peaceful with my family around!"

"Look, there's Stephie!" The twin D.J. was leading broke free and raced toward Stephanie.

"Careful, Nicky!" Stephanie sat up as Nicky plowed right into her lounge chair.

Alex begged Aunt Becky to set him down. He raced after Nicky. Becky and D.J. hurried after him.

"Wow, it's really going to be hot today!" Aunt Becky said. "You were smart to ride your bike over early, Steph. We decided we'd better get here early, too, before the crowd."

"Good thinking," Stephanie told her.

"Will you watch the twins while we get settled?" Becky asked.

"Sure." Stephanie nodded.

D.J., Becky, and Michelle grabbed three empty chairs and pulled them closer together. They piled all their things on top.

"I want to go in the water," Alex exclaimed.

"Me too!" Nicky agreed. They each grabbed one of Stephanie's hands and tried to pull her to her feet.

Stephanie laughed. "Hold on, hold on! Your mom is coming right back to take care of you."

Becky pulled off her cover-up and hurried back to the twins. "Thanks, Steph. Guess I'll see you later," she added as the twins tugged her toward the shallow end of the pool.

"Hey, Cassie's here! See you!" Michelle waved as she rushed off to meet her best friend.

"Steph, can I borrow some sunblock?" D.J. appeared at Stephanie's chair.

"Sure." Stephanie handed her the tube, and D.J. began to spread the lotion over her shoulders.

"I guess Rick hasn't shown up yet, huh?" D.J. asked, looking around the pool.

"No." Stephanie shook her head. She had told D.J. what happened the night before, after she'd woken Rick's grandmother.

D.J. had calmed her down. She made her wait until morning to call him again.

"If Rick doesn't show up soon, I'll have to call his grandmother's house again," Stephanie said.

"Call, but don't leave more than two messages," D.J. told her. "Boys hate it when you bug them too much!" D.J. spotted a college friend and hurried off.

"I agree with D.J.," Kayla told Stephanie. "Rick knows you want to talk to him. The next move should be his. Otherwise he might get mad and spend even more time with Rene."

"That's crazy!" Anna shook her head. "Where do you get these weird ideas?" she asked Kayla.

"I hate playing those kinds of games. Girls should be direct and honest with guys."

"Oh, no," Kayla whispered. "Here comes Rene!"

Stephanie stared as the Flamingoes marched into the pool area. Rene spotted Stephanie. She poked Alyssa and said something Stephanie couldn't hear. Alyssa and the other Flamingoes looked at Stephanie and laughed.

Rene and Alyssa strolled over. The other Flamingoes followed.

"Stephanie! You look so bright and perky today. I bet you had a good, long sleep last night." Rene yawned. "I barely slept. We were all out late. Big party last night, you know."

Alyssa grinned. "Yeah, too bad all you Club Stephanie losers went home right after the picnic. We all hung out at the diner with Rick, Chad, and Mike."

"And some other guys, too," Rene added. "Too bad you couldn't be there. But then, you weren't invited!" She laughed as if she'd just made a hilarious joke.

"We don't mind," Stephanie answered with a big smile. "After all, we're going to have major fun today."

"You are? How?" Rene asked.

"Don't you remember?" Stephanie asked. "Today's the day you get to model your new pink shower caps!"

Rene blinked in surprise. But she forced a smile back on her face. "Oh, come off it, Stephanie," she said. "That was all a big joke."

"Sure. It wasn't a serious bet," Alyssa added.

"Sure, it was," Stephanie replied. "And we're totally serious about it."

Rene tossed her head. "Well, we don't happen to have any pink shower caps with us. So too bad."

"No problem." Stephanie grinned. She reached under her lounge chair and pulled out the plastic shopping bag. "Allie and I picked up nine matching shower caps this morning. There's one for each of you!"

Stephanie reached into the bag and grabbed one of the hideous pink shower caps. She held it out to Rene.

Rene stared at the cap. Her mouth dropped open in horror. "I'm not wearing that—that *thing*," she sputtered.

"You'd better wear it, Rene," Darcy told her. "Everyone at the pool knows about our big bet. If you don't wear the cap, you'll really look like a bad sport."

"Yeah. Everyone will say you're chicken," Kayla added. "You wouldn't want that, would you?"

Rene glared at all of them. She snatched the cap

from Stephanie's hand and pulled it over her blond ponytail. She handed caps to Alyssa, Mary, and Julie—the other members of the swim team. They pulled them on. The enormous caps stuck out over their ears and flopped onto their foreheads. They all looked ridiculous.

Stephanie tried not to laugh. Darcy snickered. Allie and Kayla held their hands over their mouths, covering giggles. Anna laughed out loud.

A little kid running by stopped dead in her tracks. She stared and pointed. "Look, Mommy!" she said in a clear, loud voice. "Those girls think the pool is a bathtub!"

A bunch of older teens sitting nearby snickered. Rene turned almost as pink as her shower cap.

Stephanie grinned. It felt great to see the Flamingoes humiliated for once!

"All right, Stephanie—you win this one," Rene declared. "But you won't win what really matters." Her blue eyes narrowed to a squint. "You'll never win Rick!"

CHAPTER

3

◆ ◀ ▸ ◆

Stephanie felt her face flame red. "Well, you . . . I . . . ," she stammered.

"You still lost the race," Darcy quickly put in.

"Right! And you still have to wear these caps," Anna added. She began handing the rest of the shower caps to the other Flamingoes.

Darah stared at the cap in her hands. "You've got to be kidding, Rene!" she exclaimed.

"Well, Alyssa and I aren't wearing these caps alone," Rene retorted.

Darah shook her head. "Forget it, Rene! I'm not wearing this."

"Me either," Tina added. "I didn't even swim in your dumb race! No way am I going to be part of your stupid bet!"

"Yeah—me either," Tiffany declared. She threw her shower cap onto the ground. So did Tina, Cynthia, and Dominique.

Rene glared at them all in fury. Then she began to pull off her own shower cap.

"Hold it," Stephanie told her. "You *were* on the swim team, Rene. You have to wear it. That was our deal, remember? Whoever lost the relay race has to wear a shower cap to the pool for a whole day."

"Fine," Rene snapped. "I can be a good sport, you know." She grabbed Alyssa's arm. "Let's go," she ordered.

"Where are we going?" Alyssa asked as Rene dragged her away.

"To change our lifeguard schedules." Rene pointed to the shower cap on her head. "No way are we going to sit on the lifeguard stand wearing these!" Rene and Alyssa hurried off.

Stephanie and Allie slapped a high five.

"Flamingoes in pink shower caps!" Kayla crowed in delight. "I knew this would be a great day."

"Yeah. If only I could make up with Rick, it would be even better," Stephanie murmured.

"You should try to call him again, right now," Allie said.

"To tell you the truth, I'm kind of scared to,"

Stephanie admitted. "I already called four times. What if he knows I called? What if he was there all along but told his grandmother to say he wasn't home?"

"He wouldn't do something like that," Allie told her.

"Sure, he might. That note really hurt his feelings," Stephanie said.

"If you think about everything that could go wrong, you'll never get anywhere," Kayla said.

"She's right, Steph," Darcy added. "It isn't like you to be scared."

"Maybe not, but I *am* scared," Stephanie said. *They just don't realize how much losing Rick really hurts,* she thought.

She took a deep breath and stood up. "Okay, I'll do it," she announced. "I'll call his house one more time."

"Good luck," Allie told her.

Stephanie hurried to the pay phone in the clubhouse and dialed Rick's number. His grandmother answered the phone.

Stephanie took a deep breath. She had to work hard to keep her voice from wobbling from nerves. "Uh, this is Stephanie Tanner calling," she said. "May I, um, please speak to Rick, please?"

I sound like a jerk! she thought. *I'd better get control of myself!*

"I'm sorry, Stephanie," Rick's grandmother, Mrs. Summers, answered. "But Rick isn't here. He and Austin left early this morning."

"Well, do you happen to know if he's coming to the pool today?" Stephanie asked.

"Oh, he can't, dear," Mrs. Summers replied. "He and Austin are gone. They went to visit their mother."

"What?" Stephanie blinked in shock.

"Yes, she's performing a big role in a new play," Mrs. Summers explained. "It's touring all over California. Rick won't be back until the tour ends."

Stephanie felt her heart sink. "When will that be?" she asked.

"Not for weeks," Mrs. Summers told her. "The play is running for the rest of the summer season."

"The whole summer?" For a minute, Stephanie couldn't speak. Rick was gone? And he wasn't coming back?

How will I ever explain what happened with the note? She felt a burst of panic.

"B-But," she began to stammer. "I . . . don't understand. He never said anything about going away. . . ."

"It was a surprise to me, too," Mrs. Summers

23

said. "I had no idea he missed his mother so much. But Rick insisted."

"Mrs. Summers, do you have a phone number where I can call Rick?" Stephanie reached into her backpack for a pencil and a scrap of paper.

"Phone number? Well, you know, the theater group moves around so much. They do a play in one town and then move on. His mother usually calls here," Mrs. Summers explained.

"But didn't she leave a number at all? Like for emergencies?" Stephanie was beginning to feel desperate.

"Well, I think she did. Hold on." Stephanie heard Rick's grandmother opening and closing a few drawers.

"I'm sorry," Mrs. Summers said a moment later. "I can't find the number. But I'm sure Rick will call sometime. Give me your name, and I'll have him call you back."

"But . . ." Stephanie hesitated. *But what if he doesn't want to call me back?* she thought.

Stephanie recited her phone number. "Please, Mrs. Summers, tell him it's really important that he calls me!" Stephanie said.

"I will," Rick's grandmother promised.

Stephanie thanked her and hung up the phone. She wandered slowly back to the pool.

"Stephanie?" Allie asked. "Are you all right?"

"What happened?" Anna demanded. "Did you talk to Rick?"

"No." Stephanie felt as if a big hollow place was inside her. "He's gone. He won't be back for the rest of the summer. I can't call him. And I don't think he'll return my call." She gazed at her friends. "You guys, what will I do?"

CHAPTER

4

◆ ◀ ◆ ◆

"Hurry with those paper masks," Stephanie told Anna and Darcy. "The campers will be here in about two seconds!"

Anna, Darcy, and Stephanie were the first to arrive at the pool. They were busy setting up an arts and crafts project.

"Don't you just love Mondays?" Darcy grinned as three or four campers raced toward the picnic area. "The kids are always so excited at the start of a new week!"

"Yeah." Stephanie was thoughtful a moment. "It's hard to believe that two whole weeks have gone by—since Rick left, I mean."

Darcy and Anna exchanged looks of concern.

26

"You're still thinking about him a lot, aren't you?" Anna asked.

"I can't help it," Stephanie admitted. "I think about him every hour of every day."

"Do you suppose his grandmother ever gave him your message?" Darcy asked.

Stephanie shrugged. "I don't know."

She had called Mrs. Summers several times, asking if Rick had called yet. Finally his grandmother told Stephanie that Rick *had* called—but he didn't want to speak to Stephanie. He even told his grandmother not to give Stephanie his phone number.

"I'm really sorry, Steph," Allie told her. "But at least we're busy with camp. That must help keep your mind off Rick a little."

"It helps," Stephanie said. She grinned again. "Especially when there's an extra-special camper."

"You don't mean Karin, do you?" Anna grinned, too.

Karin Carver was new at camp. She'd only been there for three days—but she'd caused trouble all three days!

Karin refused to play with the other kids. She refused to do arts and crafts. She refused to go in the water at swim time. And she refused to tell anyone why she refused to do those things.

Darcy shook her head in frustration. "If only she'd talk to one of us. Maybe we could help her."

"I'll try again today," Stephanie said.

Karin arrived a few minutes later. Janice, her baby-sitter, led her in by the hand. Janice found Karin a place to sit beside Brittany, another camper.

As soon as Janice left, Karin jumped up and sat by herself at the end of a bench. She folded her arms stubbornly over her Looney Tunes T-shirt. She glared at everyone who came near her.

Stephanie strolled over and sat down beside Karin. "Hey, Karin," she began brightly. "It's my turn to fix morning snack today. And I'm not very good at making peanut butter crackers. Do you think you could help me later?"

Karin shook her head. Her brown braids whipped against her cheeks. "I don't want to help. I want to go home," she mumbled.

Stephanie reached for Karin's hand. "You just got here! Wouldn't you like to make a scary mask with the other kids first?"

"No! I want my daddy," Karin said.

"Well, Janice will be back to pick you up when camp ends," Stephanie told her in a soothing voice. "Then you can go home. And you'll see your daddy tonight."

"I want Daddy right now!" Karin started to run

away from the camp area. Stephanie sprinted after her and scooped her up. "Whoa! Got you," she said with a smile.

"Put me down!" Karin kicked and screamed. The other kids stared at them.

"Okay, down you go!" Stephanie pretended they were playing a game. The other campers turned away. Stephanie gently placed Karin on her feet.

"Karin! Just the camper I wanted to see!" Anna rushed up with a yellow paper mask, a bottle of glue, and a trayful of glitter and feathers. "One special-delivery mask project for you!"

Karin grabbed the tray. She sat down by herself again and began making a mask.

"Thanks, Anna," Stephanie muttered. "She's not playing with the other campers, but at least she's working on a project."

Anna nodded. "I have a feeling it's going to take Karin a while to be nice to the other campers."

Stephanie tried hard all morning to get Karin to play with the other kids. But Karin refused. She clung to Stephanie.

Finally it was time for the kids to leave. Stephanie felt totally worn out. She was relieved as the parents and baby-sitters began arriving. One by one the campers left.

Suddenly Stephanie spotted Karin sitting alone

again. "Oh, no!" she exclaimed as she realized that Karin was crying.

Stephanie rushed over and dropped onto the bench beside her. "Hey, there's no reason for tears! Janice will be here any second."

"I want my daddy," Karin wailed.

Janice ran up. "Sorry I'm late," she said. "I got held up in traffic." She gave Karin a big hug. "Did you think I wasn't coming, sweetie pie?"

Karin nodded, but she stopped crying.

"Um, Janice," Stephanie began. "Karin had a really hard time again today. Are you sure she's ready for day camp?"

"Oh, yes," Janice insisted. "Her father especially wants her to spend more time with other kids."

"Well, okay," Stephanie told her. "Maybe she'll do that tomorrow."

"I'm sure she will," Janice replied. She grasped Karin's hand and led her away.

"Whew," Stephanie said when Karin and Janice were out of sight. "I hope Karin gets used to camp soon. Because I'm not sure I can get used to Karin."

Kayla and Darcy laughed. "Well, let's hit the snack shack," Kayla said. "Maybe you'll feel better after you eat."

"Maybe," Stephanie agreed.

Anna and Allie finished clearing away the last of the camp equipment. Then they all hurried to the snack shack. They bought sandwiches and drinks and carried them to an empty table.

"Hi, guys," a deep voice said behind them. "How's it going?"

"Cody!" Stephanie blinked in surprise. "What are you doing here?"

Cody James was Kayla's fifteen-year-old cousin. He had coached their swim team to help them win the relay race at the Fourth July picnic. They hadn't seen him since.

"I thought you might need more coaching," Cody teased.

"Not right now. We're too busy eating lunch," Stephanie joked back.

"But how did you get here?" Kayla asked him. Cody lived on the other side of San Francisco.

"My dad is working nearby," Cody explained. "He'll be coming here a few days a week till the end of summer. And I still have the pool pass Kayla got me when I was coaching you guys." Cody grinned. "I figured I might as well use it."

"But don't you have your own community pool closer to home?" Stephanie asked.

Cody pushed his wavy brown hair off his forehead. His cheeks dimpled, and his brown eyes sparkled. "Yeah, but I really like this place. Especially the people you meet here." He looked right at Stephanie.

Stephanie felt her cheeks flush. She knew Cody liked her. Kayla had told her at the picnic.

"You guys are hanging out at the pool this afternoon, right?" Cody asked.

"Sure," Kayla answered. "We always do."

"Great. I'm going to change. I'll see you later." Cody waved and hurried toward the men's locker room.

"Cody is so cute," Anna said.

Stephanie glanced at her in surprise. "Do you think so, Anna?"

Anna shifted her eyes. "Sure. But we all know he likes you, Stephanie."

"Right," Kayla said. "Do you think you could like him back?"

Stephanie felt uncomfortable. "I don't know. I mean, he is cute and really nice," she replied. "But I can't think about any boy right now."

Any boy except Rick, she added to herself.

Stephanie stood. "I'm going to change into my suit, too," she said. "See you guys in the locker room."

She hurried toward the clubhouse. The locker room entrance was right next to the pay phone. She hesitated.

If only Rick would speak to me again, she thought. *Maybe he won't come back to San Francisco, but at least I could explain what happened with the note. At least he would know the truth. And then, maybe—*

Sandy Kovacs tapped Stephanie lightly on the shoulder. Sandy was the activities director at the pool. "Are you all right, Stephanie? You have a strange look on your face."

"Oh, hi, Sandy," Stephanie replied. "Yeah, I'm fine. I was just thinking about something."

"Well, you're just the person I wanted to see." Sandy ran a hand through her short, reddish hair. "Did you notice the poster I just put up?" She pointed to the bulletin board across from the telephone.

Stephanie turned and looked closely at the board. She saw a huge yellow poster that wasn't there before.

She quickly read through it:

Teen Dance!
Calling all teens!
Come to a planning session for our biggest event ever!
The Say-Good-bye-to-Summer Dance
You can make it happen!
Meet at the snack shack July 23,
Wednesday afternoon at 4:30!

"I think this dance could be extra cool," Sandy told her. "That's why I want you kids involved in

33

the planning. I'll have the final say, of course, but I'll hand over most of the work to committees. We'll need a very energetic chairperson to keep everything organized." She nodded at Stephanie. "It's a big job, but I hope you'll volunteer."

"Me? Really?" Stephanie thought about it.

Being chairperson for a major dance would be a lot of work. But it felt good to know that Sandy trusted her with so much responsibility.

And it could be fun to help plan the dance— even if she wouldn't have anyone special to dance with.

Stephanie felt a new burst of excitement. Working hard would keep her busy, and keeping busy would keep her mind off Rick.

"So what do you say?" Sandy asked.

Stephanie made up her mind. "You can count on me. I'll be at the meeting. Definitely!"

CHAPTER
5

♦ ◂ ♦ ♦

"I'm glad we got seats right up front, close to Sandy," Stephanie said. She glanced around the snack shack. Wednesday afternoon's planning meeting was about to begin. The rows of seats were already crowded. Stephanie sat between Darcy and Anna on one side and Allie and Kayla on the other side.

"I can't believe how many people showed up," Allie replied.

"It's great," Stephanie told her. "This means I'll have lots of help on my committees. I'm so glad Sandy asked me to run things."

"Hurry, Alyssa, they're about to start!" Rene's voice rang across the room. Stephanie turned to see Rene and Alyssa pushing their way to the row of seats right in front of her. They were both still dressed in their red lifeguard's tank suits with red shorts pulled over them.

"I'm really too busy for this meeting," Rene complained to Alyssa. "But if we want the dance to be any good, we have to run it ourselves."

"Tell me about it," Alyssa agreed.

Rene made some other girls move aside to make room for her and Alyssa.

"Hey, wait a minute!" Stephanie said to Rene. "You're not running anything."

Rene turned around. When she saw Stephanie sitting there, she scowled. "Oh, really? Why not?" she demanded.

"Because Sandy already asked me to be chairperson," Stephanie replied.

"She never told me that," Rene said.

"Well, I—" Stephanie began. Just then, Sandy stepped up to the speaker's platform set up at the front of the room.

"Welcome to our dance planning session," Sandy began. "And thanks for coming! It's great to have such a big turnout. Because this is really *your* dance."

There were shouts of approval and applause.

"To make sure you get your ideas across, we're going to need a really special chairperson to run the committees," Sandy continued. "Someone who is organized and gets along well with people."

Allie dug Stephanie in the ribs. "That's you!" she whispered.

Sandy smiled. "I never expected so many eager volunteers," she said. "So to make this fair, I guess we should take a vote. May I hear nominations for chairperson?"

Stephanie glanced at Allie in surprise. "Nominations? I thought I already had the job!"

"I nominate Rene Salter," Alyssa called out.

Stephanie's jaw dropped.

"I nominate Stephanie Tanner," Allie quickly called.

"Thanks, Al," Stephanie whispered.

"No problem," Allie whispered back. "You deserve to win!"

Sandy wrote down both names. "Any other nominees?" she asked.

"Why would anyone else run?" Alyssa asked. "Everyone knows Rene is the best!"

There were shouts of laughter and a spattering of applause. Stephanie felt her cheeks flame in embarrassment.

"I don't believe this!" Anna muttered. "Now Rene's going to try to take over the dance, too!"

"Those Flamingoes take over everything," Kayla complained.

"Maybe she'll lose," Allie whispered back. "There are hardly any Flamingoes here to vote for her."

There was a sudden burst of noise from the back of the room. The doors were flung open, and the rest of the Flamingoes marched inside. They had brought about a dozen other friends—kids who had barely shown up at the pool all summer.

"Oh, no!" Darcy groaned. "I should have known they'd do something sneaky like this!"

Stephanie quickly glanced around the room. She saw lots of kids she knew from school. Many of them didn't like the Flamingoes. She was sure they'd vote for her. But would she have enough votes to beat Rene?

"Okay, then. Let's vote," Sandy said. "All those in favor of Stephanie?"

Sandy counted the hands that shot into the air. "Twenty-five for Stephanie. Those in favor of Rene?"

Stephanie turned—and groaned.

"Thirty-six for Rene!" Sandy wrote the totals in her notebook. "Well, you're the new dance chairperson, Rene. Congratulations."

Darcy poked Stephanie in the side. "I'm almost sure Mary and Tina raised both hands," she said.

"There's nothing we can do about it now,"

Stephanie replied. "We'll look like really bad losers if we tell Sandy."

Anna scowled. "This is so unfair! I wish someone would build a big rocket ship and send those Flamingoes to the moon."

"Quiet, people!" Sandy called. "Please sign up with Rene for the different committees. Let's all work together to make this dance really special, because . . . because—" She paused for a long moment. The room grew quiet as everyone exchanged curious looks.

Sandy gave a sheepish smile. "Well, I don't know exactly how to say this," she finally went on. "But this dance should be really special, because—it will be our last dance ever. I just found out that the whole community center is closing at the end of the summer."

"You mean, no more pool? But why?" Stephanie stared at Sandy in shock.

She tried to imagine what summer would be like with no pool. Her family had been coming here every summer since she was a little kid. There were volleyball and softball leagues that met on the playing fields. And there were often parties or dances and movie nights in the fall and winter.

All around her, kids were sitting in stunned silence or calling out questions. Sandy raised her hands for silence.

"I just heard from the city Parks Department last night," Sandy said. "So it's a surprise to me, too."

"But this is the only pool around here," someone behind Stephanie complained.

"I know." Sandy looked as upset as Stephanie felt. "But the Parks Department feels there isn't enough money available to keep the center running anymore."

"What can we do?" someone called.

"Well, there's going to be an open meeting about it this Friday. Anyone who wants to can come," Sandy replied. "And watch the bulletin board. I'll post more news if I hear any." She forced a smile. "Anyway, let's not worry about it now. Just think about what a great dance we'll have. Okay?" Sandy ended the meeting and hurried out of the room.

"I can't believe this," Stephanie murmured.

"Where will we hang out without the pool?" Darcy asked.

They wandered out of the clubhouse and crossed automatically to the pool. Stephanie gazed at the sparkling blue water. She turned to take in the smooth green lawns and the tall trees that shaded the picnic area. She could hardly believe it might all be shut down.

Allie placed a hand on Stephanie's arm. "Don't

feel too bad, Steph," she said. "Lots of kids would rather have you be chairperson for the dance."

"Dance?" Stephanie shook her head. "I'm not worried about who's running the dance anymore," she told Allie. "Let Rene be chairperson. The only thing that matters now is saving the pool."

"But how can we do that?" Allie asked.

"Yeah," Darcy added. "The Parks Department decides that kind of stuff, not us. There's nothing we can do. We're just kids." Kayla nodded.

"That's not true. There's always something," Stephanie told her.

"Like what?" Allie asked.

"Like we can all show up at that meeting on Friday, for a start," Stephanie said. "Maybe we'll get some ideas. There has got to be a way to keep the pool open. And I'm going to find out!"

CHAPTER
6

"No offense, Steph," Darcy said. "But you looked awful at camp today."

"I know," Stephanie said. "But at least it's Thursday. Only one more day of camp this week." She slid her tray onto the picnic table next to Darcy's.

Stephanie had made an extra effort to get Karin involved in camp all week. But nothing seemed to work.

"I felt kind of awful all morning," Stephanie replied. "I didn't get much sleep last night. All I could think about was saving the pool."

Allie shot her a sharp look. "Is that really all you thought about?"

"No," Stephanie admitted. "I thought about Rick a lot, too."

She couldn't help glancing across the pool. Rene sat in the lifeguard chair, chatting with a bunch of guys and girls.

Rene was lucky, in a way, Stephanie realized. Rene liked Rick, too, but she didn't seem to mind half as much that he was gone.

"That's Rene's dance planning committee," Allie told them.

"She probably has the entire dance planned already," Kayla added. "It will be called Pink Paradise, and even the guys will have to wear pink. Pink shirts and pink jeans!"

Anna burst out laughing.

"Don't laugh," Allie said. "That's just the kind of thing Rene might do."

"Sandy won't let her get away with anything too weird," Stephanie told them.

They stopped talking as Rene hurried past, carrying a big poster.

"Hey, Rene, what's the poster all about?" Darcy called.

"You'll see," Rene replied with a sly smile. She headed for the clubhouse. Stephanie saw her hang the poster on the bulletin board.

"Who wants to go see what Rene's up to now?" Darcy asked.

"It's probably a list of dance rules a mile long," Anna cracked.

"Well, I'm dying of curiosity," Allie said. "Come on."

They headed over to the bulletin board. Rene grinned at them as they gathered around. She had tacked the poster smack in the middle of the board, covering a bunch of smaller notices. The poster was printed in purple ink on pink paper:

Summer's End Fantasy Formal
Couples Only

End your summer with the most romantic event ever!
Invite your favorite guy or girl
to dance in the moonlight!

Date: Saturday, August 26
Time: 8 P.M. till ?
Place: Patio at the snack shack
Tickets: $50 per couple
Tickets go on sale soon!

"What? You can't do this!" Stephanie exploded. "You can't make our one big dance for couples only!"

"This dance should be open to anyone who wants to go," Darcy said angrily.

"And it shouldn't cost a fortune, either!" Allie added.

"And formal?" Kayla groaned. "Who wants to buy an expensive, long dress to wear?"

"Sandy couldn't have approved all this," Stephanie said.

"Oh, no?" Rene lifted her chin. "We need to raise money, don't we?" she demanded. "So making the dance formal and charging a lot is a way to raise money."

"Come off it, Rene! It probably takes megabucks to keep this place running," Darcy replied. "Fifty-dollar tickets won't raise that kind of money."

"Says who?" Rene smirked. "You guys are probably just worried that you won't be able to find dates."

"Like you have a date already," Anna said.

"I just might," Rene shot back. "And a really special date, too," she added, glancing at Stephanie.

Could she mean Rick? Stephanie felt a jolt of fear run through her. Could Rene somehow have found out Rick's phone number and already called and asked him to the dance?

Or worse—what if Rick had called her!

"Who are you talking about, Rene?" Stephanie asked.

"As if you didn't know," Rene replied.

"Are you saying that Rick called and asked you?" Stephanie demanded.

"Well, he didn't ask *you*, did he?" Rene raised her eyebrows.

"No. But I don't believe he called you, either," Stephanie replied.

Kayla stepped between them. "I don't care who has a date or not," she said. "You can't get away with this, Rene. You can't make up all these rules for the dance."

"Can't I?" Rene smiled sweetly. "I'm the chairperson, remember?" Rene strolled into the locker room.

Stephanie gave Allie a worried look. "You don't think she really has a date with Rick, do you?" she asked in a low voice.

"I don't know," Allie answered. "Would Rick come all the way back here just for a dance?"

"Well, the dance is the last weekend of summer," Stephanie pointed out. "His mom's tour will have ended by then. I guess he *could* come back for the dance."

"Never," Anna vowed. "Rene is lying. I bet Rick never called her."

"Yeah—and he still might call you," Allie added in a hopeful tone.

Stephanie shook her head. "Forget that, Allie. It's

been three weeks. If he *was* going to call, he would have called already."

"Well, I'm not looking forward to this dumb dance anymore," Darcy declared. "Not if it's formal!"

"I agree," Anna added. "I don't think we should even have a dance. It makes more sense to scrap it and have some kind of fund-raiser for the pool instead."

"What kind of fund-raiser?" Allie asked.

"I don't know." Anna shrugged.

"Hey, wait a minute!" Stephanie suddenly exclaimed. "I just had the greatest idea. We could *combine* the dance with a fund-raiser. We could have a dance-a-thon!"

"A what?" Kayla asked.

"It's like a marathon, only it's a dance," Stephanie explained. "First people make pledges. They agree to pay a certain amount for every hour we can dance."

"So you mean it's like a contest to see who can keep dancing the longest?" Kayla looked confused.

"Exactly," Stephanie told her. "People might pledge, say, five dollars an hour for one couple. If they danced for five hours, they'd make twenty-five dollars."

"That's nothing," Darcy said.

"No, but we could get hundreds of pledges,"

Stephanie explained. "And some people might pledge ten dollars, or even more."

"Wow. If we had a hundred fifty-dollar pledges, we'd make five thousand dollars!" Allie exclaimed.

"And we might get much more than that," Stephanie pointed out.

"We could really raise a pile of money!" Anna declared. "This really is a great idea, Steph!"

"Let's run it by Sandy and see what she thinks," Allie suggested.

Sandy was thrilled. "I can't wait to get started on this idea," she told them. "Parents and friends can help, too. It can be a true community project."

"That's right," Stephanie agreed. "I know my family will want to be part of this." She paused. "And, of course, this means there won't be any rules about bringing dates, right?"

"Right." Sandy eyed her thoughtfully. "You know, Stephanie, you and Rene are both incredible workers," she said. "You both have strong personalities and tons of energy. You could accomplish so much if you worked together, as a team."

As if Rene would ever agree to work with me, Stephanie thought.

"I think we're better off this way," she told Sandy. "Rene is chairperson. But Club Stephanie will work as hard as we can to make the dance-a-thon a total success!"

Sandy thanked them, and Stephanie and the others hurried out of her office. "I can't wait to start getting pledges," Stephanie said.

"This is so exciting!" Allie grinned. "You were right again, Steph—there *is* a way to save the pool!"

"Yeah, but this is more than a way to save the pool," Kayla added.

"It is?" Stephanie asked.

"Sure! It's also a great way to put Rene in her place!" Kayla beamed. "Everyone will know the dance-a-thon was your idea."

"You're right!" Stephanie smiled. "Club Stephanie rules again. And this time, Rene better watch her step!"

CHAPTER
7

"Good-bye, Karin! See you on Monday!" Stephanie waved as Karin left camp with Janice. Karin didn't wave back—or smile. Stephanie sighed. "Another week gone. Can you believe it's the middle of August already? And Karin still won't talk to anyone but me!"

"Face it, Steph," Anna said. "No one could get to her. She's impossible!" Anna shook her head. The beads on her earrings jangled together.

Stephanie tried not to smile. "But Anna, you think anyone who doesn't love arts and crafts is impossible—or crazy," she teased.

Anna giggled. "I guess that is sort of true," she said. "But still, Karin is kind of . . . extreme."

"Yeah, I know," Stephanie replied. "But I'm sure there's a reason for the way she's acting."

"I don't know how you can stand it," Darcy said. "All she does is cling to you or sit by herself. Why don't you just give up?"

"I can't." Stephanie shook her head.

"Well, except for Karin, it was a fun week," Allie said as they all headed for the snack shack.

"Yeah, but I'm glad it's the weekend tomorrow," Kayla said. "Two whole days to ourselves! I'm going to swim, swim, swim!"

"Not me," Allie declared.

"Oh, what are you going to do? Snack, snack, snack?" Kayla teased. They all knew how Allie loved sweets.

Allie and Stephanie found an empty table in the snack shack. They waited at the table to save their seats while Kayla, Anna, and Darcy left to get the food. They were gone only a few minutes when Anna came running back. Darcy and Kayla were right behind her.

"Steph! Allie! Look at this!" Anna waved a copy of the local newspaper over her head. "You won't believe what the Flamingoes have done now!"

Anna sat at the table, and the others crowded close. Stephanie stared at the newspaper over Anna's shoulder. "What am I supposed to be looking at?" she asked.

"Front page; you can't miss it," Anna replied.

"Oh, no!" Stephanie's eyes opened wide as she spotted a huge picture that took up almost the entire front page. It was a group photo of all the Flamingoes, with Rene right in the middle. Under the photo was a huge headline: Local Teens Fight to Save Community Pool!

Stephanie read the rest of the article out loud. "Teen dance chairperson Rene Salter has come up with a unique way to raise money to save the popular local pool from closing. A fund-raising dance-a-thon will take place at summer's end. Local teens will gather pledges from the community, paying for every hour couples continue dancing.

" 'I had to do something,' said the fourteen-year-old Ms. Salter. 'The community center is so special to so many people. I knew that everyone was counting on me—so I came up with a way to raise money and have fun, too!' "

Stephanie threw down the paper in disgust. "This is the worst thing she's done yet!" she declared.

"That was your idea, Steph, and everyone knows it!" Darcy declared.

"How did she even find out about it?" Allie asked.

"I don't know," Stephanie began to say.

"Wait . . . Rene was right there when we were talking about the formal dance, remember?"

"That's right," Allie said. "She tacked up the poster, then went into the locker room."

Darcy snorted. "You mean she *pretended* to go in the locker room. She must have hidden in the doorway and listened to our whole conversation!"

"That sneak!" Kayla fumed. "She stole your idea and called the newspaper before we even thought of it!"

"Well, we should call the newspaper back right now and make sure you get the credit, Stephanie," Anna said.

"We can't," Stephanie told her. "Even if they believe us, what could they do? Print another front-page article to say they listened to the wrong kid?"

"They might," Anna insisted.

"But we can't start a fight in the paper over who said what," Stephanie told her. "It's best to leave it alone. It doesn't really matter who gets the credit. It's more important to get publicity for our dance-a-thon."

"Well, this still stinks," Darcy declared.

"I know," Stephanie replied. "I hate being beaten by the Flamingoes again, too."

And by Rene, she added to herself. *It's bad enough*

that she took Rick away from me. Now she's even taking my ideas!

"Wait, there's more," Anna said. "Show her what you found on the bulletin board, Darcy."

"You're not going to believe this, either," Darcy said. She held up a flyer for everyone to see:

IMPORTANT NOTICE!!
Attention, Dance-a-thon Contestants!
All dates and dresses must be approved
by the dance committee to make sure
they meet our high standards of good taste!

"Am I reading this right?" Stephanie demanded. "The Flamingoes have to approve who we bring to the dance?"

"That's crazy," Darcy declared. "I'm bringing Billy Golden, from school. And that's final."

"Yeah, and Jack Kramer asked me to be his partner," Kayla said. Jack was another eighth-grader who hung out at the pool. "I would never ask the Flamingoes for their permission to dance with him—or anyone!"

"And how about checking what we wear?" Allie stared at the notice in astonishment. "Nobody will show if she keeps this up!"

"What will she come up with next?" Kayla wondered.

"We'll probably have to buy our dresses at Flamingo-approved stores," Anna cracked.

"This is totally outrageous," Allie declared. "Sandy will never let her get away with this."

"Neither will we," Stephanie added. "Come on—let's find Rene and clear up this whole thing!"

Stephanie stormed across the patio toward the pool. Allie, Kayla, Darcy, and Anna followed. They were halfway there when they spotted Rene and Alyssa heading for them. Rene's face was bright red. Stephanie had never seen her so angry.

"I suppose this is your idea of a joke!" Rene fumed. She shoved a flyer under Stephanie's nose.

"My idea of a joke?" Stephanie stared at her. "You mean, your idea of a power trip. You're not telling anyone what we can wear to a dance!"

"Or who we can dance with!" Darcy added.

"What are you talking about?" Rene demanded.

"Stop acting so innocent," Alyssa said. "You know you only did this to get back at Rene because she was voted chairperson. You *made* Sandy put you on the committee!"

"I did not!" Stephanie glared.

"And Rene wrote this notice," Kayla added.

"Who, me?" Rene shook her head. "I did not! You did!"

"Hold on—you mean you really didn't write it?"

Stephanie looked at Rene and Alyssa more closely. They actually seemed to be telling the truth.

"Of course we didn't write it," Rene snapped. "We'd never do a juvenile thing like that."

Stephanie opened her mouth to remind Rene of all the other juvenile tricks she had played, then shut it again.

"Besides, who else wants to get the Flamingoes in trouble with Sandy?" Rene demanded.

"You think you'll get in trouble for this?" Darcy asked.

"We already did," Alyssa declared. "Sandy was furious. Now we have to tell everyone they can come to the dance without a date if they want to and wear whatever they want."

"We're being punished for something we didn't even do!" Rene crossed her arms over her chest.

"Well, I don't know who did it," Stephanie said.

"Anyway, it serves you right," Darcy added. "You guys stole the credit for Steph's dance-a-thon idea. So it doesn't bother me if you get punished for somebody else's flyer."

Rene flushed. "How do you know we didn't think of a dance-a-thon, too?" she asked.

Stephanie rolled her eyes. "Listen, Rene. Saving the pool really matters to me. So let's agree to forget about this flyer business. We need to start getting pledges for the dance-a-thon. And Sandy wants us to work together."

Rene snorted. "Why should we work with you? You sure don't have the right contacts to get big pledges."

"Oh, no, her dad's only the host of a TV show," Darcy said in a sarcastic tone. "No chance of publicity there!"

"It's true," Stephanie said. "My dad and Aunt Becky plan to make announcements about the dance-a-thon on their show for the next few weeks. That should help bring in plenty of pledges."

"That's not fair!" Alyssa exclaimed.

"This isn't a contest between us," Stephanie pointed out.

Rene's eyes narrowed. "Well, we plan to work for our pledges," she said. "You know, ringing doorbells and hitting the mall to talk to people. We can't take any shortcuts."

"Shortcuts?" Stephanie stared at Rene. "Who's taking shortcuts? We'll ring doorbells and hit the mall, too. Then we'll see who gets more pledges."

"Fine," Rene snapped. "We'll see who raises the most money, you or us!"

"Fine!" Stephanie snapped back. Rene and Alyssa stormed off.

"Okay, the mall opens at ten tomorrow morning," Stephanie told her friends. "Who's coming with me?"

CHAPTER
8

♦ ◄ ♦ ♦

"This is so weird," Stephanie said in a low voice. "I've never been the very first one at the mall before."

"It does feel kind of spooky," Allie agreed.

Stephanie scanned the entrance lobby. The mall was practically empty. Storekeepers were still rolling up the gates that covered their plate glass windows at night.

"Here come Darcy and Anna," Allie said. Stephanie saw them struggling through the main doors, carrying a folding table.

"Hey, you guys!" Stephanie waved them over. "The mall manager found us the perfect spot for our table."

"Just point us to the place," Darcy said.

"Over there, by that big fountain." Stephanie pointed a little way down the wide hallway. She and Allie followed Darcy and Anna. They set down their table and paused to catch their breath.

"I also made us a big sign," Anna said. She lifted a wide poster so they could read it: Help Save Our Community Pool! Pledge to Support Our Dance-a-thon!

Stephanie examined the careful, bright lettering. "That's a really great sign, Anna."

"Thanks," Anna replied. "So are we ready to get started?"

Stephanie nodded. "I thought we'd split up. Allie and I will stay here at the table. Anna can cover the far end of the mall, and Kayla and Darcy can work this end, by the big department store. After lunch, we'll all switch."

"Sounds good to me," Anna said.

"Too bad there are only five of us," Darcy added.

"Nope—make that six!" Stephanie grinned and pointed at the main entrance. Cody and Kayla were just arriving.

"Hi, guys!" Kayla called as they approached the table. "I told Cody about the pledge drive, and he said he had to help. I hope it's okay with you."

"Okay? It's great," Anna blurted. "I mean, we can use all the help we can get."

"Well, I can only stay till lunchtime," Cody said. "My dad's picking me up then. But I wanted to help."

"That's okay," Darcy told him. "I was just saying we could use more people. We need to gather tons of signatures and pledges."

Stephanie showed Cody and Kayla the pledge sheets she and Allie had copied that morning.

"There's a place for a name, address, and phone number, plus the amount each person is pledging," Allie explained.

"But there's no space for comments," Anna said. "Won't people want to tell the Parks Department how they feel about the pool?"

"Why? It takes time to write down comments," Cody said. "The important thing is to raise money—not scare people away."

"You are so wrong," Anna told him. "People feel important when they get to express how they feel about an issue."

"They can go home and write letters to the Parks Department if they want," Cody argued.

"What if they want to make comments? I can't tell them it's not allowed," Anna said.

"I'm telling you, it's a waste of valuable time!" Cody's voice rose.

"Well, I don't see it like that," Anna said in a

calm voice. "I think everyone's comments are really valuable. And—"

"Hold it, you two!" Stephanie interrupted. "You both have good points. But can't we just let people do what they want?"

"Sure. If they have a comment, fine," Darcy said. "If not, also fine."

"I guess," Cody said.

Anna shrugged.

"Okay, so here are your pledge sheets and extra blank pages for comments." Stephanie divided the pile of papers between Anna and Cody.

I better keep Anna away from Cody, she thought. *They do nothing but argue with each other!*

"Cody, why don't you take the middle of the mall?" Stephanie said.

"I could use some help," Anna murmured. "Cody and I could work together."

Cody shrugged. "Okay. Whatever you say." He and Anna hurried off.

"What was that all about?" Kayla asked.

"You know Anna," Stephanie replied. "She wouldn't be Anna if she didn't tell people exactly what she thought."

"I guess." Kayla grabbed a pile of pledge sheets. Darcy stuffed her pockets with extra pens. "I'm ready. Let's go," she said.

The morning went quickly. Stephanie was

amazed by the number of people who wanted to pledge their support.

"I'm glad to tell the Parks Department how I want my tax dollars spent," one woman told them. "You kids deserve a place to go when you're not in school."

"We sure agree with that," Stephanie said as the woman wrote down her comments.

"It's amazing," Allie muttered as the woman strode away. "Everyone has really strong feelings on this." She lifted the heavy stack of papers.

"Anna was right about that," Stephanie said. "We may need even more comment sheets."

Allie checked her watch. "Hey, it's getting late. When do we stop for lunch and trade places?"

"How about right now?" Stephanie replied. "I'm starved." She signaled to the others. Darcy and Kayla decided to keep working and eat lunch later. Anna and Cody said they would take over the table.

Stephanie and Allie hurried toward the escalators that led to the upstairs food court.

"Hey, what's all the commotion?" Allie asked.

The food court was crowded with people. Music was loudly playing, and a girl's voice echoed through a loudspeaker.

"It's your pool, too! Help save it today," the voice announced. "Make your voice count!"

Stephanie gasped. Rene!

"Oh, no, not again!" Allie muttered. They edged closer to the crowd. A huge, colorful pink banner was strung across the food court. In silver glittering letters, it said: Dance-a-thon to Save Our Pool! We'll Dance Our Hearts Out for You! Please Open Your Hearts for Us and Pledge!

"What a great slogan," Stephanie muttered.

"Hey, Stephanie. What are you doing here?" Alyssa pushed her way through the crowd.

"We're getting pledges, same as you," Stephanie told her.

"Well, the Flamingoes have taken over the food court," Alyssa told them.

"But we were here first," Allie said.

"Who cares? You don't own the mall." Alyssa shrugged. "We're doing great. How are you doing?"

"Terrific," Stephanie said. "We probably have more pledges than you. And I bet we'll do even better this afternoon. So you can have the food court."

"Oh, right. You know we'll beat you guys. But you can pretend you know what you're doing." Alyssa hurried back to the Flamingoes' pledge table.

"Let's eat fast and get back to work," Stephanie

said. She and Allie grabbed burgers and drinks and gulped them down in record time. They hurried downstairs to tell the others about the Flamingoes.

"They were really getting a ton of signatures," Stephanie finished.

"Well, we can get just as many as they can," Kayla replied. She turned to Darcy. "Let's grab a bite to eat and then head over to the multiplex. The first shows are starting soon."

"Sure. We'll get tons of signatures there," Darcy agreed. She and Kayla hurried off.

Cody turned to Stephanie. "Can I speak to you for a minute—alone?" he asked.

"Sure." Stephanie followed Cody to a marble bench near the big fountain.

"I've been thinking," Cody said. "I really want to help save the pool. And I'll be glad to go to the dance-a-thon. But it would be a lot more fun if you were my partner."

"Oh!" Stephanie didn't know what to say.

"I'd be a great partner," he teased. "You know that swimming keeps me in great shape. I bet I could dance all night!"

Stephanie laughed. Cody was so sweet and fun, too. Why shouldn't she go with him? It was about time she faced the facts—she was never going to see Rick again this summer. He was out of her life forever.

"I wanted to ask you sooner," Cody said. "But I know you like that guy Rick, so . . ."

"We broke up," Stephanie said. "I mean, he left town."

"Well, does that mean you say yes?" Cody gave her a hopeful look.

"Sure. I mean, yes," Stephanie said.

"Great!" Cody grinned. "Listen, I have to run. But we can make more definite plans about this some other time, okay?"

"Okay." Stephanie watched him go. Then she hurried back to the pledge table.

"What was that all about?" Anna asked.

"Cody asked me to be his partner at the dance-a-thon," Stephanie answered.

"And? What did you say?" Kayla asked.

"I said yes," Stephanie replied. "Why not? It'll be fun dancing with Cody."

Since there isn't a chance I could dance with Rick! she added to herself.

"Oh, no!" Anna blurted. "Stephanie, you *can't* go to the dance with Cody!"

CHAPTER

9

◆ ◀ ◾ ◆

Anna flushed in embarrassment. Stephanie stared at her in surprise.

"Why shouldn't I go to the dance with Cody?" Stephanie demanded.

"I just meant—uh—that you shouldn't give up on Rick," Anna stammered. "We all know you really like him. I mean, what if he comes back and finds out you're going to the dance with someone else?"

"I don't think that's going to happen," Stephanie said. "He's away for the rest of the summer, remember? And he obviously doesn't care about me."

"Yes, but, um, I just think you should wait a

little longer," Anna said. "Before you rush into anything you might regret."

"She's not going to marry Cody, Anna," Darcy said. "She's only going to dance with him."

"And speaking of the dance, we need to discuss something really important—like what we're all going to wear," Kayla said.

"Anything but pink," Darcy joked.

"I think we should all show up in our pajamas, just to drive the Flamingoes crazy," Stephanie said.

They all cracked up.

Stephanie snuck a glance at Anna. She was laughing with everyone else.

I wonder if she was really upset that I'm going to the dance with Cody? Stephanie thought. *But why would she be?*

She shook her head. It made no sense.

Too strange, she thought. She decided to forget all about it.

But on Monday at camp, Anna was still acting strange. Stephanie helped her set out the paper and paints for the campers' morning art project.

"Why don't I mix the paints while you explain what the kids should do?" she suggested to Anna.

"No! I'll handle it," Anna snapped.

Stephanie shot her a curious look. "Well, okay. There's no need to bite my head off."

Anna looked up. "It's just that I know how I like the paints mixed," she said.

"Whatever." Stephanie hesitated. "Have I done something to make you mad at me, Anna?"

"Of course not. Why?" Anna asked.

"I just get that feeling," Stephanie said. "I mean, you've been avoiding me all day. But every time I turn around, you're watching me."

Anna flushed. "That's crazy! You're imagining things," she said. "Everything's fine."

Maybe I am just imagining things, Stephanie thought.

"Another fun day at camp?" a boy's voice asked.

"Cody!" Stephanie was surprised to see him there. He was wearing a blue tank top and black shorts that showed off his tan. His dark sunglasses made him look extra cool.

"You keep showing up at the oddest times," Stephanie said.

"I thought I'd see if you were going to the snack shack for lunch," he said.

"Not until camp is over," Stephanie replied. She glanced at her watch. "We have forty more minutes left."

"No problem. I'll wait for you over there," Cody said.

"You mean you don't want to stick around and help with the finger painting?" Stephanie teased.

Cody grinned. "I think I'll pass. But I'll see you later." He waved and hurried off.

Stephanie watched him go. "Cody is incredibly nice," she remarked to Anna. "Don't you think he's easy to talk to?"

"I thought you were going to help me with the paints," Anna snapped.

"But you said—" Stephanie blinked at her in surprise.

"What?" Anna demanded.

"Uh, nothing," Stephanie told her. "Show me what I should do."

Anna and Stephanie mixed up the paints. Darcy, Allie, and Kayla helped hand out paper to all the kids. Soon the campers were busy rubbing their fingers across the papers.

Stephanie couldn't help laughing as she watched. "It's a good thing we used washable paint," she told Allie. "The kids are practically covered!"

"They're really having fun," Allie replied. "Even Karin."

"I hope she's finally getting more comfortable at camp," Stephanie said.

"Well, a lot of good things already happened this summer," Allie reminded her. "We ran Club Stephanie all by ourselves, and it was a big success."

"That's true. And I even earned enough money to buy myself the new bike I need," Stephanie added. "Now, if only we could get Karin to love camp. And get tons more pledges than the Flamingoes!"

"You left out one thing—dates for the dance, like you and Darcy and Kayla," Allie teased.

"I thought you and Anna wanted to go by yourselves," Stephanie said in surprise. "I thought you wanted to be able to dance with any guy who's there."

"Well, that's probably what we'll do," Allie replied. "But I'd love to have a date I cared about."

"But Cody isn't the guy I really want to go with," Stephanie reminded her.

"That is so totally unfair!" Anna blurted.

Stephanie stared at her. Anna's face had turned pink. "What's unfair?" Stephanie asked.

"It's unfair for you to go with Cody since you don't really like him," Anna stammered. "I mean, you only said yes because you can't go with Rick. But what if someone else really wants to go with Cody?"

"Like who?" Kayla asked.

Anna shrugged. "How would I know?"

Allie looked closely at her. "That person wouldn't be you, would it, Anna?"

"No!" Anna nearly shouted. Her face turned even deeper red.

Oh, no! I've been so dense! Stephanie thought. Now she understood why Anna had been acting so weird. Anna liked Cody. She wanted to go to the dance with him—and she was jealous of Stephanie!

"Oh, Anna! I didn't know you liked Cody," Stephanie said. "You should have said something. I would never have agreed to be his date."

"Thanks," Anna muttered. "I guess I have been acting pretty weird, trying to hide the way I feel. But telling you about it wouldn't do any good."

"Why not? What do you mean?" Kayla asked.

Anna shrugged. "He still wouldn't ask me. He doesn't even know I exist."

"Oh, he knows you exist!" Stephanie grinned, thinking about Anna and Cody arguing in the mall. "He just has no idea that you like him."

"Well, then we have to change that," Kayla said.

"Right!" Stephanie nodded. "We'll find a way to make him notice you, Anna."

"But you already agreed to go to the dance with him," Anna pointed out.

"People break dates all the time," Stephanie told her. *They even leave town to get away from you!* she couldn't help thinking. "Besides," Stephanie went on, "how do you know that Cody wouldn't rather go with you?"

"Yeah, I can really picture you two together," Allie told Anna. "I think Stephanie is right."

"Now all we have to do is convince Cody." Stephanie frowned in thought. "Come on. It's time to dismiss the campers. Then we all have a date at the snack shack—to start Operation Anna and Cody!"

"There he is." Kayla pointed across the patio. "He saved us a table."

Anna stopped walking. "You know, I don't think I'm hungry after all," she said. "You guys go ahead. I'll see you later."

"What? Anna, don't tell me you're scared!" Stephanie glanced at her in surprise.

"That is so *not* like you!" Kayla exclaimed.

Stephanie grabbed Anna's arm. "Come on, it'll be fine," she told Anna. "You have to start talking to him sometime."

"Does it have to be now?" Anna asked.

"Listen, this won't be so hard," Stephanie said. "First I'll find a way to break my date with Cody. Then we'll get the two of you talking."

"But not arguing," Kayla added.

"That might be hard," Anna admitted.

"Just try to agree with whatever he says," Stephanie told her. "And remember, you don't have to make a date today. Okay?"

Anna took a deep breath. "Okay. I'll try—but don't expect too much."

Kayla marched Anna up to Cody's table. "Here we are!" Kayla announced.

"Didn't I get you great seats?" Cody asked.

"Uh, very great," Anna replied. She stared blankly at Cody, as if she couldn't think of one more thing to say. She shot Stephanie a pleading look.

"Uh, Cody, there's something we should talk about," Stephanie began. "It's about the dance. I was wondering—"

"I know! Which dance steps are my best?" Cody stood up and held out his arms as if he were doing an old-fashioned waltz. "I'm good at everything," he joked. "Except the macarena!"

Stephanie shook her head. "No, Cody, really. I'm serious. What would you think if—"

"If we beat the pants off the others?" Cody danced over to Stephanie. He wrapped one arm around her waist and swung her around. "Don't worry, we will! We'll make those Flamingoes eat our dust." He laughed and gave her a big hug.

Stephanie glanced at Anna. Anna looked miserable. "Listen, Cody, I—" Stephanie tried again. She was surprised when she heard Allie gasp.

She turned—and saw something that made the smile fade from her face.

Rick was standing right in front of her!

CHAPTER
10

◆ ◀ ◢ ◆

"Rick!" Stephanie broke away from Cody.

Rick gave her a disgusted look and started to walk away.

"Rick, wait!" Stephanie ran to catch up with him. "Rick, wait—please, you don't understand!"

Rick didn't slow down.

"At least give me a chance to explain," Stephanie pleaded. "That letter you got—it wasn't from me. I didn't write it. It was a fake. I would never say those horrible things. Please believe me, Rick!" She swallowed hard. "I missed you so much!"

Rick paused. He turned and glared at Stephanie. "Oh, I saw how much you missed me," he said. "You know, one of the reasons I came back here

74

was to talk to you. I wanted to give you a chance to explain. But I guess I should have saved myself the trip."

"No, you're wrong! Cody is a friend! You don't understand. . . ." Stephanie grabbed his sleeve. Rick shook himself free.

"I understand fine," he said. "I didn't want to believe them, but I guess they were right after all."

"Who was right? About what?"

"Cynthia and Alyssa." Rick lowered his eyes. "They told me about you and . . . and that Cody guy."

"But it's not true!" Stephanie's eyes widened in horror. "Cody and I are just—"

"Friends?" Rick demanded. "Yeah, right. I saw him with his arm around you. You didn't look like friends to me."

"But we were only dancing! It didn't mean anything. We—" Stephanie began.

"Save your breath," Rick cut in. "You'd better get back to your boyfriend." He paused. "I wish I never came here again." Rick hurried away.

Stephanie turned around and saw Cody, looking embarrassed.

What a disaster! she thought.

Cody strode quickly away from the snack bar. Stephanie hurried to catch up to him. "Cody, I'm sorry," she called.

Cody stopped and waited until she was next to him. "I guess that was the guy you broke up with, huh?"

"Yeah," Stephanie said.

"What was he doing here?" Cody asked.

"I don't know. He didn't say how he got back or anything." Stephanie felt tears well up in her eyes. How could she begin to tell Cody all about the switched letters? "Anyway, there was something important I needed to explain to him. But . . ."

"But what?"

"But he didn't give me a chance," Stephanie answered in a whisper. "He wouldn't listen, Cody. He wouldn't let me talk. I guess he was too upset."

"You mean because he saw the two of us together?" Cody asked.

Stephanie nodded.

"I get it," Cody said. "So I guess I helped mess things up with him again."

"It wasn't your fault," Stephanie said. "It's just that, well, the Flamingoes told him that we're going out."

"What? Why did they do that?" Cody asked in surprise.

"Because Rene likes Rick. And it was a good way to make trouble for me," Stephanie answered.

"They'll do anything!" Cody exclaimed.

"They've done worse things than that," Stephanie told him. "You don't know the reason Rick broke up with me—the Flamingoes gave him a note that said I thought he was a terrible kisser!"

Cody stared. "You're really angry about it," he said slowly. "I guess that means you still care about him a lot."

Stephanie shrugged. "I guess so."

Cody shook his head. "Wow. He's pretty lucky. I mean, he believes a bunch of Flamingoes instead of you, and you still like him."

"I can't help it, Cody," Stephanie whispered. "Maybe we'd better not go to the dance-a-thon together. Okay?"

"Sure. Okay." Cody forced a grin, but Stephanie could tell he was really hurt.

"I'm sorry," Stephanie told him.

"Sure." Cody ducked his head and hurried away.

What a mess, Stephanie thought as she watched him go. *Rick hates me, and now I've hurt Cody, too!*

Attention, All Dance-a-thon Dancers!
All girls must attend a special workshop:
How to Do Your Makeup Right!
The Flamingoes will teach you
to look good in publicity photos!
Time and date to be announced.
Sign up now!

"They're at it again!" Stephanie exclaimed.

Darcy, Anna, and Kayla crowded close to her for a better look at the flyer.

"Allie and I found these on the picnic tables when we got to camp this morning," Stephanie explained. "I can't wait to see what Sandy says about them."

"Are you kidding? She'll go ballistic!" Darcy said. "Don't those Flamingoes ever learn?"

"But they swore they didn't put up the last flyer," Allie reminded her.

Darcy laughed. "As if I believe that!"

Stephanie nudged her. "Well, you can ask them yourself. Because here they come now. And they don't look happy."

Rene and Alyssa stormed across the picnic area. Rene held a crumpled-up flyer in one hand. She waved it angrily at Stephanie.

"Are you crazy or something?" Rene exploded. "How could you try this again! You just don't give up, do you?"

Stephanie sighed. "I know you don't believe me, Rene. But I had nothing to do with this flyer, either."

"And I think you Flamingoes really wrote it," Darcy added.

Rene turned to her. "Well, you think wrong! Sandy wanted us all to work together," she added.

"But obviously somebody around here is trying to get me kicked off the dance committee."

"Was Sandy mad at you?" Stephanie asked.

"No, actually," Alyssa reported. "She was annoyed that the sign said you must attend. But she thought learning to apply makeup wouldn't hurt anyone."

"Sandy said that?" Stephanie asked.

"That's right," Rene replied with a smug grin. "So your little trick backfired."

"It wasn't my trick," Stephanie said again.

Rene shrugged. "Anyway, we *are* going to do a workshop. But don't bother signing up," she told Stephanie. "I doubt if makeup could make you look better—and Rick likes his dates to look really good."

Rene grabbed Alyssa. They turned and hurried away just as the first campers began to arrive.

Allie squeezed Stephanie's arm. "Don't mind her, Steph. That was a dumb insult."

"I already forgot it," Stephanie said. "Look who's coming to camp!"

CHAPTER
11

◆ ◀ ▪ ◆

Stephanie nodded toward the arriving campers.

"Austin!" Allie exclaimed. "He's back!"

And he reminds me so much of Rick! Stephanie thought.

She wondered if Rick had looked like his little brother Austin when he was small. Did Rick have Austin's wide blue eyes and golden curls? Rick's eyes were still blue, of course, but not as huge as Austin's. And Rick's hair was wavy now, not curly.

Stephanie couldn't stop her gaze from wandering over to the pool. She could see Rick sitting on the lifeguard's chair. It was a windy morning, and his blond hair was ruffled.

Stephanie felt as if there was a big hole inside her. It hurt so much to see him and to know that he was mad at her. If only she could make him listen long enough to understand! He still had no idea that the Flamingoes split them up on purpose.

If only I could get one more chance to explain, Stephanie told herself.

But then, that might not do any good. Rick really liked Rene. He liked the Flamingoes. He thought they were fun to hang out with. Most of the boys thought so. Only Cody understood how nasty the Flamingoes could be.

And now Cody is mad at me, too! Stephanie tried not to groan out loud. The dance was in less than ten days. How could she possibly fix things before then?

"Stephanie!" Austin threw himself at her and wrapped his arms around her.

"Austin! It's great to have you back at camp!" Stephanie gave him a big hug. "Are you back for good?" *And is Rick?* she added to herself.

"I think so," Austin said. "Visiting my mom was boring."

"Well, camp is never boring," she told him with a grin. "Especially when you're around!"

"But the pool is going to close," Karin said. She stood close to Stephanie. Austin eyed her with distrust. Karin stared back.

"Who are you?" Austin demanded.

"This is Karin Carver," Stephanie explained

when Karin wouldn't answer. "She's our newest camper."

Austin shrugged. "Is the pool really closing?" he asked.

"Maybe," Stephanie said. "Some people do want to close it. But we're going to find a way to keep it open."

"Rick can do it," Austin said. "He's a lifeguard. He can do anything."

Stephanie forced a smile. "Rick is great, Austin. But he can't save the pool by himself."

"That's true, but all you guys can help," Kayla said.

"We can? How?" Austin asked.

The other campers gathered around. Kayla and Stephanie explained all about the dance-a-thon. They showed the kids pledge sheets and asked them to take the sheets home to their friends and families.

"And you can all pledge to support your favorite dancer," Stephanie went on. "Me, Allie, Kayla, Anna, or Darcy."

"I choose you!" Austin shouted.

"Thanks, Austin." Stephanie patted his hair. *I wish your brother felt the same way!*

"My grandma will give lots of money," Austin bragged.

"My daddy will give more," Karin burst out. Stephanie glanced at her in surprise.

"No, he won't!" Austin stepped close to Karin.

"Yes, he will! He's rich, rich, rich!" Karin shouted in Austin's face.

"Hold it, you guys! Stop arguing!" Stephanie told them, trying to hide her smile. It was great that Karin was finally talking to someone—even if she was arguing!

"It doesn't matter if you're rich or not," Stephanie went on. "Everyone can pledge something. Even a few dollars will help. Okay?"

"Okay," Karin and Austin both mumbled.

"And I have another idea," Anna announced. "Let's all paint special banners about the dance-a-thon. Then we'll hang them all over town so every single person will know how to save the pool! Do you like that idea?"

"Yes!" all the campers shouted—except Karin. She was silent and moping again, Stephanie noticed.

The other kids began to chatter with excitement. Anna and Kayla divided them into groups to begin the project. Darcy and Allie helped letter the banners. Then the kids began to paint.

"Are you okay here, Karin?" Stephanie asked.

Karin sat on the end of a bench by herself. She

leaned over a banner, painting in a giant letter *L*.
She nodded, barely paying attention to Stephanie.

Stephanie strolled over to Austin. She grinned at
the way he stuck his tongue out of the corner of
his mouth as he painted. She sat on the bench beside him.

"So Austin, tell me more about your trip," she
said. "Like, um, what did Rick do while your mom
was busy acting?"

"Nothing. Sometimes we watched cartoons on
TV," Austin said.

"Did Rick have fun doing that?" Stephanie
asked.

"No. He was grouchy. He didn't even want to
play with me," Austin answered.

Stephanie leaned closer. "How come he was so
grouchy?"

Austin shrugged. "I don't know."

"Maybe he missed his friends," Stephanie said.
"Did he ever talk about me, for instance?"

Austin shrugged. "I think so. Maybe."

Stephanie felt a tiny burst of hope. After all, Rick
had come back before his mom's tour ended—and
he had said he wanted to talk to her.

*But then I blew it by being with Cody when he
walked in!* Stephanie could have kicked herself.
There's got to be a way to get through to him.

The kids worked on the banners all morning.

They stopped only for their swim lesson. Rick was still on duty when Stephanie helped herd the campers over to the pool. He pretended not to notice her, but she could feel his eyes on her as soon as her back was turned.

Her brain raced, trying to think of something to say.

"Stephanie, help," a muffled voice cried. She turned to find Karin with her T-shirt stuck halfway off. It covered her whole face.

Stephanie bent over to help Karin and heard Rene's voice right behind her.

"Hey, Rick! I heard you were back! How's it going?"

From the corner of her eye, Stephanie saw Rene climb onto the lifeguard's chair. She sat close to Rick.

She knows I can hear every word she's saying! Stephanie fumed. She willed herself not to look at them. She folded Karin's T-shirt.

"I'm so glad you decided to come back early," Rene went on. "Especially because of the big dance-a-thon."

"Yeah, Sandy told me all about that," Rick said. "I can't believe anyone wants to close this pool."

"Well, they won't," Rene declared. "Not if I can help it!" She leaned even closer to Rick.

"Listen, I need a special partner," Rene told Rick. "One who can really dance. Interested?"

Stephanie caught her breath. Rene was asking Rick to be her date!

"You're asking me to go to the dance with you?" Rick turned to stare at Stephanie. She quickly dropped her eyes, pretending she couldn't hear what he was saying.

"We'd make a great couple," Rene said. "How about it?"

"Sure," Rick said. "Why not?"

Stephanie could hardly believe her ears.

Rick said yes? She didn't want to believe it. She felt a sick knot form in her stomach.

It can't be all over, she told herself. *Rene won't win this easily! Rick has to find out the truth about Rene—and he will!*

CHAPTER

12

◆ ◂ ◆ ◆

"Any luck talking to Rick?" Allie asked.

Stephanie sighed. "No. He hasn't spoken to me in the last four days. And now there are only six days left till the dance," she complained. "I guess it's totally hopeless."

Stephanie waved her pledge sheet as she and Allie trudged through the mall. "Sign up here! Make a pledge to support your community pool!" she called.

"Only six days left!" Allie added. "Make your pledge before the dance-a-thon!"

Busy shoppers hurried past. It was Sunday and their last weekend to gather pledges at the mall. Not many people were stopping to sign up.

"I guess everyone who's going to pledge already did," Allie said.

"Guess so." Stephanie brightened. "But we've done pretty well, anyway. Altogether, Club Stephanie has over three hundred dollars pledged for every hour each of us dances."

"And there are five of us. So let's see . . ." Allie concentrated. "If we dance from seven o'clock to midnight, that makes—over seven thousand dollars!"

"And don't forget all the grown-ups who are getting pledges, too," Stephanie reminded her.

"I know we can come up with the money we need," Allie said.

Stephanie nodded. "And we'll beat those Flamingoes, too," she added. "I bet Club Stephanie will bring in twice as many pledges as they do."

They continued through the mall. Kayla and Darcy were in charge of the table near the mall entrance. Anna and Cody were covering the opposite end of the mall.

"Any news on Operation Cody and Anna?" Allie asked.

"Nope." Stephanie shook her head in frustration. "Those two are impossible! I don't think they'll ever get together."

"At least they're spending time together today,"

Allie said. "I wish Anna would just get it together to ask Cody to be her date."

Stephanie giggled. "Isn't it funny that Anna is actually afraid to ask him?"

"Yeah. She's not usually afraid of anyone!" Allie gave Stephanie a thoughtful glance. "Maybe you should have kept your date with Cody. At least then you'd have a partner."

Stephanie shook her head. "Anna really wants to go with him," she said. "I know how it feels when you like someone and you see them with someone else."

"Oh. Right," Allie said. "Sorry."

"Don't feel sorry for me," Stephanie told her. "It just makes me really want to get Anna and Cody together." She glanced up. "Hey—here come Anna and Cody now! And Darcy and Kayla are with them."

"Why did they leave the table?" Allie wondered.

"I don't know. Let's find out. Hi, guys," Stephanie called. "What's up?"

"We wanted to get up close to the entertainment," Cody answered.

"What entertainment?" Allie asked.

"There's a TV camera setting up over by the multiplex," Darcy told them. "We think they're going to film a commercial or something."

"Maybe we'll get to be extras," Kayla said. "Isn't it exciting?"

"Yeah. Let's hurry!" Stephanie grabbed Allie's arm. They all rushed to the plaza in front of the movie theaters. About fifty people milled about. Stephanie and the others made their way to the front of the crowd.

"Oh, no!" Stephanie exclaimed. "Do you see what I see?"

"Flamingoes!" Allie groaned. Rene, Alyssa, Cynthia, and a bunch of the other Flamingoes were clustered around a man holding a microphone.

Stephanie frowned. "They're not making a commercial," she said.

"Then what are they doing?" Kayla asked.

"I'm not sure," Stephanie replied. "But that's a TV crew." She pointed to the cameraman. KWUJ was printed across his video camera in big white letters.

Rene was talking to the man who held the microphone. "He looks like a TV reporter," Darcy said.

"How about if we stand right here, with the movie entrance behind us?" Rene asked in a loud voice. She glanced around to make sure everyone was watching her.

"What's happening?" Cody asked the man standing next to him.

"It's an interview for Bay TV," he answered.

"Okay—this is a take," the reporter told the cameraman. The camera pointed directly at Rene.

"Do you think the Flamingoes will raise enough money to save the pool?" the reporter asked.

Rene smiled right at the camera. "Oh, yes! You wouldn't believe how fast the pledges are coming in," she said. "Everyone loves this pool. They'll do anything to help! I personally already have over two hundred dollars of pledges for each hour I dance. And the other Flamingoes are doing great, too."

Allie poked Stephanie in the side. "Did you hear that?" she whispered. "Rene has nearly as many pledges as all of us put together!"

"Well, Rene, you're getting lots of publicity for the dance-a-thon," the reporter went on.

"Yes. I knew it was a wonderful idea the moment I thought of it," Rene replied. "We hope that your broadcast will help remind everyone in the city that there's only a short time left to pledge."

The reporter turned to the camera. "Did you hear that, San Francisco?" he asked. "Hurry to the mall, or call in your pledge now."

He held the microphone out to Rene, and she recited a phone number.

"Okay, that's a wrap," the reporter called.

"Let's get some shots of Rene and her friends in other parts of the mall," the cameraman suggested.

Rene spotted Stephanie in the crowd. She hurried over. "Can you believe I'm going to be on television?" Rene gloated.

"I can't believe you're still saying the dance-a-thon was your idea," Stephanie muttered.

"We are going to get so many pledges!" Cynthia waved a pledge sheet in front of Stephanie's face.

"We'll be able to buy a whole new pool with all this money!" Alyssa added.

"Too bad you guys couldn't drum up such great publicity," Rene said. She smirked at Stephanie. "But you'll have the whole mall to yourselves for the rest of this afternoon."

"We will? Why?" Allie asked.

"Because after I finish my interview, I have to go shopping." Rene gave Stephanie a phony sweet smile. "I need a really special dress for my big date with Rick. I want to look my best, since he's the cutest guy at the pool. But then, you know that, don't you?"

Stephanie barely managed to force a smile. *I will not let her see how angry she makes me*, she told herself.

Rene gave a little wave as she hurried away. The rest of the Flamingoes followed the camera crew.

Some of the crowd of onlookers followed them. The rest drifted away.

"Rene just makes me so furious!" Stephanie exclaimed the minute they were gone.

"She's pretty hard to take, all right," Darcy agreed. "But she's right about one thing—we might as well pack it in for today." She folded her pledge sheets and tucked them into her backpack. "The Flamingoes are going to get the rest of the pledges at the mall, not us."

"I guess you're right." Stephanie shook her head in disappointment. "I guess there's no way Club Stephanie is going to beat the Flamingoes now."

For a moment, they were all silent.

Kayla sighed. "Let's not mope about it."

"I agree," Darcy said. "Anyone want to hang out around here?"

Stephanie glanced at the movie posters hanging next to them. "Why not catch a movie?" she suggested.

"Good idea," Darcy said.

"Just make sure Cody and Anna sit together!" Allie whispered.

"Exactly what I was thinking," Stephanie whispered back. She turned to Cody. "This must be your lucky day," she told him. "You get to go to the movies with five great girls."

"Sounds good to me." Cody grinned. "Which movie do you guys want to see?"

Anna turned and examined the movie posters lining the wall. "How about *Heartbroken?*" she asked.

"*Heartbroken?*" Cody made a disgusted face. "Isn't that one of those British movies?"

"Yes, a historical romance. I just love them!" Anna sighed.

"Give me a break," Cody muttered. "I can never understand what anyone's saying. They put me to sleep. But hey! *Android Hunter* is playing."

"*Android Hunter?* How can you stand to watch movies like that?" Anna demanded. "They are totally violent—and brainless."

"So? They're not supposed to be serious," Cody argued. "And they say this one has incredible special effects."

"Ugh! All those dumb exploding cars and fireballs." Anna shook her head in pity. "Typical guy flick."

"At least there's some action," Cody retorted. "The biggest thing that happens in those British movies is when somebody knocks over a teacup."

"But the characters have intelligent conversations," Anna said. "They don't just grunt and groan when they get blown to pieces."

Stephanie and Allie exchanged a look of dismay.

This was supposed to bring Anna and Cody together?

"Cool it, you guys," Darcy told them. "We could do something else."

"Yeah," Kayla added. "Maybe a movie isn't such a good idea after all."

"Sure, it is," Stephanie told them. "As long as we pick a movie we all want to see."

"Well, I guess I could see *Android Hunter*—if everyone else wants to," Anna said.

Yay! Stephanie silently cheered.

"And I guess I could survive one British flick," Cody said. He grinned, flashing his dimples. "If someone translates for me!"

Anna and Cody exchanged a smile. They walked toward the ticket booth together.

Allie nudged Stephanie in excitement. "You see? We thought Anna and Cody didn't have a chance. But there is hope for them after all."

"Well, yeah, that's great," Stephanie said.

Allie gave her an impatient look. "You don't understand, Steph. I mean that there may still be hope for you and Rick, too."

"How?" Stephanie asked. "There is no way to make Rick even talk to me."

"There has to be," Allie told her. "Promise me you won't give up on Rick?"

"Allie, that's crazy," Stephanie began. "There is no way that Rick—"

"Promise," Allie insisted. She gave Stephanie a huge grin.

"Okay," Stephanie finally said. "I promise. I won't give up on Rick!"

CHAPTER
13

♦ ◄ ♦ ♦

"I just saw Sandy," Stephanie announced the next morning as she arrived at camp. "She told me that the Flamingoes' TV campaign already helped bring in tons more pledges."

"I don't know if that's good news or bad news," Allie said.

"Well, it's rotten news for us," Anna joked. "But great news for the pool!"

"You're right, Anna," Stephanie said. "Besides, I'm listening to what you told me, Allie."

"What's that?" Allie asked.

"Never give up hope," Stephanie repeated. "We might still beat the Flamingoes at getting pledges."

Though I have no idea how, she thought.

"Enough about the Flamingoes," Anna declared.

"Here come the campers—let's get them right to work."

In a few minutes, all the kids were organized and hard at work. They knew this was the very last week of camp, and they were more excited then ever about finishing their banners for the dance-a-thon.

"Too bad you guys are too little to stay up and watch the dance," Stephanie remarked to Austin.

"I don't care," Austin said. He sat at the same table as Karin. Karin was sitting by herself on the end of the bench, as usual.

"Well, that's a nice letter *D* you're painting, Karin," Stephanie told her.

"I'm not painting a dumb letter," Austin piped up. "I'm painting a picture of my mom. She makes a good dancer for our banner, doesn't she?"

"Yeah. She looks great," Stephanie replied.

"I'm making her pretty, because she is." Austin stuck his tongue between his lips as he painted on long blond hair.

"That's a terrific picture," Stephanie praised. She smiled at Karin. "Why don't you try a picture of your mom?" she asked.

Karin's eyes widened. They filled with tears. Karin jumped up from the table.

"Karin! What's wrong?" Stephanie looked at her in surprise.

Karin turned and ran.

"Karin, wait!" Stephanie yelled. "Come back!"

She chased after Karin and finally caught up with her near the clubhouse.

"Whoa!" Stephanie flung an arm around Karin's waist. She dropped onto both knees to be able to look into her eyes.

"Karin! Please, tell me what happened," Stephanie begged. "What got you so upset?"

Karin started crying. "You told Austin his picture was pretty!" she said between sobs. "I hate his picture!"

"Why do you hate it, honey?" Stephanie asked.

"He was just bragging," Karin said.

"But Austin's mom is far away. He misses her," Stephanie said. "That's why he bragged about her."

"My mommy is far away, too," Karin blurted.

"Well, I know you miss her," Stephanie began. "But she'll be back soon, just like Austin's mom."

"No, she won't." Karin's voice dropped to a tiny whisper. "She died last year."

Stephanie felt tears sting her eyes. "Oh, no," she murmured. "Oh, Karin. I'm so sorry. I know how you feel."

"No, you don't," Karin said.

Stephanie gave Karin a quick hug. "But I do," she told her. "Because my mommy died, too."

Karin stopped crying. She looked at Stephanie in surprise. "She did?"

Stephanie nodded. "When I was a little girl, just about your age. I still remember how scared I was. And how much it hurt."

Karin stared at Stephanie wide-eyed.

"It hurt a lot," Stephanie told her. "But my mommy didn't want to leave me. And I'm sure yours didn't want to leave you. So don't ever be mad at her. And don't be mad at Austin, either. Or other kids."

"Why not?" Karin demanded.

"Well, because they might have lost someone, too. Austin doesn't have a daddy around anymore," Stephanie said.

"Did his daddy die?" Karin asked.

"No. But his parents got divorced when he was a little baby. His daddy went to live far away," Stephanie said. "So he just has a mommy. I bet he thinks you're lucky to have your daddy."

"I love Daddy," Karin said.

Stephanie hugged her. She stood up and smiled. "Now, why don't you go finish your banner. Okay?"

Karin smiled back. "Okay!"

She ran back to the picnic area. Stephanie watched her go, then turned to follow.

Rick was standing in the clubhouse doorway,

dressed in his red lifeguard shorts and tank top. Stephanie opened her mouth to say something. *But what should I say?*

For a moment, they just stared at each other.

Finally Rick cleared his throat. "I—uh—you handled that really well," he said. "You sure have a magic touch with kids."

"Yeah, I'm great with little kids," Stephanie managed to say. "I just wish I had the magic touch with big kids."

"You do?"

"Yeah," Stephanie said. "Because if I did, then I could get one big kid to listen to the truth."

"Were you telling the truth when you said you didn't send that note?" Rick asked.

Stephanie took a deep breath.

Finally! she thought. *Finally he's going to listen to me!*

"Of course!" she nearly yelled. "I never wanted to break up with you."

"Then why did you start going with that other guy?" Rick demanded.

"I didn't, Rick," Stephanie said. "We really are just friends. Anna likes Cody, not me."

"Really?" Rick asked in a hopeful tone.

"Honest," Stephanie told him. "I wanted to explain it all to you. But you wouldn't believe me."

"Try me now," Rick said.

"Well, I did write you a note," she began. "But the Flamingoes switched it for that horrible note you read."

"I can't believe they would do that." Rick sounded amazed.

"Look, I know you like Rene and her friends," Stephanie told him. "But you don't know how mean they can be."

"They're great to me," Rick said. He was thoughtful for a moment. "Though they did insist that you were going with Cody."

"And I'm not," Stephanie declared. "Cody's a great guy, but . . . but I like someone else."

Their eyes met.

"So what did your note say?" Rick asked. "The one I was really supposed to get?"

Stephanie's cheeks turned red. "I, uh, I just said that I liked you a lot. More than I liked any boy before. And, uh, I said I hoped we could start over again."

"Wow." Rick shook his head. "I'm sorry I didn't believe you, Steph."

Stephanie gazed at him. "But you believe me now?"

"Yeah." Rick reached for her hand. "I missed you. And deep down, I couldn't believe you wrote that note. It just wasn't like you."

"I'd never say something that nasty," Stephanie told him. "Especially because it isn't true!"

Rick laughed. "Thanks. I guess that's why I decided to come back here—that and the fact that Austin was bugging the heck out of me. He really wanted to get back to camp—and to his Stephanie." He gave her a smile that made her feel warm all over.

"I really missed you, too, Rick," Stephanie said.

Rick shook his head in disbelief. "I acted like a real jerk," he said. "But Rene—" He broke off. "Oh, no!" He smacked his forehead.

"What?" Stephanie asked.

"Rene! I said I'd go to the dance with her." Rick squeezed Stephanie's hand. "Wow. I really want to go with you."

"I wish you could," Stephanie said.

"I will," Rick said. "All I have to do is break my date with Rene."

"That might be harder than you think," Stephanie told him.

Rick made a face. "I have all this week to do it," he said. "Five whole days. Believe me, I won't need five days to break one date."

"You're right." Stephanie gazed happily into Rick's eyes. "No one needs five days to break one simple date."

CHAPTER
14

◆ ◀ ◢ ◆

"It's hard to believe that Club Stephanie is almost over for the summer," Darcy said.

The campers were gathered in a big circle while Anna read them a story. They were waiting for their parents and baby-sitters to pick them up.

"Here we are, only two days left, and we're wondering if there will ever *be* another summer of Club Stephanie!" Allie shook her head in dismay. "Isn't it weird, Steph? Steph?" she repeated.

Stephanie blinked and stared at Allie. "Huh?"

Allie and Darcy exchanged an amused look. "I guess you were thinking about Rick again," Allie said.

Stephanie gave them a sheepish grin. "Yeah. Sorry."

"Still dreaming about her big date!" Allie teased.

"You must feel great that Rick is breaking his date with Rene today," Kayla said. "It really proves how much he wants to take you."

"I don't even blame him for stalling," Allie said. "I know you wanted him to do it before now. But I'd stall, too. I wouldn't want Rene mad at me."

"I think he was just trying to find a way to do it without hurting her feelings," Stephanie said. "I mean, we don't think that Rene has feelings. But Rick does."

"Well, don't worry. I'm sure Rick will handle it exactly right," Kayla said.

"Me too," Stephanie agreed. She knelt down and began gathering up the last of the camp supplies to put away. Allie knelt beside her.

"It's too bad things aren't working out as well for Anna and Cody," she said.

"I know. She really wants to ask him to the dance, but she still doesn't have the nerve," Stephanie replied. "I think she's really mad at herself."

"At least they seemed to get along better during the movie on Sunday," Allie said. "They only argued a couple of times."

Stephanie giggled. "That's practically a record for them! If only we could find another chance to get them together."

Darcy glanced at her watch. She clapped for attention. "Okay, kids," she announced to the campers. "Pair up with your buddies. Get ready for dismissal!"

The kids began to line up to go meet their parents and sitters. Suddenly Karin broke away from the group. She ran across the picnic area toward the clubhouse.

"Oh, no!" Darcy exclaimed. "What now?"

"I'll get her," Stephanie said. She broke into a run, chasing after Karin.

"Karin, come back," she called. She noticed a man wearing a dark business suit striding toward them.

Karin threw herself into his arms. "Daddy! Daddy, you came!" she yelled.

Mr. Carver scooped her up. He gave her a big, noisy kiss. Karin giggled.

Stephanie grinned as she watched them.

"You bet I came," Mr. Carver said. "I promised, didn't I? Don't forget, we have a date today. We're going out to lunch together."

Karin noticed Stephanie. "My daddy came to see me, Steph," she announced, beaming with pride.

Mr. Carver set Karin on her feet. "Go wait for me on that bench over there, okay, sweetie?" he asked. "I'll get you in one minute." Karin ran to sit on the bench.

Mr. Carver studied Stephanie with interest. "So

you're the famous Stephanie," he said. "Karin talks about you all the time."

"Really? Well, I think she's great," Stephanie replied.

"You know, I just got back from a long business trip," Mr. Carver explained. "But I wanted to come tell you how happy I am with your camp. Karin really trusts you. And she really loves camp now. In fact, she's like a different girl these days."

"I'm really glad," Stephanie said.

"But you know, I'm curious about something," Mr. Carver said. "I'm dying to know what all these notices are."

"Notices?" Stephanie asked.

Mr. Carver nodded. "Yes, Karin told me she had to paint big notices to go up all over town."

Stephanie laughed. "Oh, that! The kids made banners for our fund-raiser. We're holding a dance-a-thon on Saturday."

Mr. Carver threw back his head and laughed. "Karin called it a dance-a-*phone*. I had no idea what she was talking about!"

Stephanie laughed, too, but then her smile faded. "Actually, it's a pretty serious situation," she said. "They're going to close this whole community center at the end of the summer. We're trying to save it."

"You must feel pretty strongly about it," Mr. Carver said.

"We all do," Stephanie said. "We may not raise enough money. But we still want the Parks Department to know that we care enough to fight for the center."

"Good for you," Mr. Carver said. "Uh—I think someone needs you." He nodded across the picnic area.

Stephanie looked up to see all the Club Stephanie counselors standing by the clubhouse. Anna was waving at her furiously.

"I'd better go. Nice to meet you." Stephanie said good-bye and hurried to meet Anna.

Anna lifted a piece of pink paper in the air. "Hurry, Steph. You've got to see this!" she called.

Stephanie realized that it was another flyer, signed by all the Flamingoes.

"What's going on now?" she asked.

"Those Flamingoes are up to something new!" Anna declared. She handed Stephanie the flyer:

ATTENTION!
All dancers in the dance-a-thon
must pass a tango test
before being allowed on the dance floor!

Stephanie's mouth dropped open in astonishment.

"This is incredible!" she burst out. "They have some nerve, making up more dumb rules!"

"I know," Anna said. "Isn't it amazing?"

Kayla covered her mouth with both hands, trying not to laugh. Anna poked her in the side.

"Of course, they'll insist they didn't make this flyer, either," Darcy said. "But it had to be them."

"Or else it's someone who hates the Flamingoes as much as we do and wants to get them in trouble," Stephanie said.

Stephanie noticed Kayla's face flush bright red. Suddenly Kayla and Anna burst out laughing.

"You guys! It was you, wasn't it?" Stephanie demanded.

"Okay, okay, we confess. It was my idea," Anna said, grinning.

"But I helped her do it," Kayla added.

"You guys are too much!" Stephanie, Allie, and Darcy burst out laughing, too.

"Well, we only did it the first time because someone had to teach those birdbrains a lesson," Anna said.

"Yeah. We never seem to beat them at anything. We couldn't take it anymore," Kayla added.

Anna nodded. "And getting them in trouble

with Sandy seemed like the only way we'd ever get revenge."

"Well, I've only got one thing to say to you two," Stephanie declared, fighting to keep her expression serious. "I wish I'd thought of it first!"

Allie had tears in her eyes from laughing so hard. "I wonder if they'd think this flyer was funny," she said.

"Let's ask them," Stephanie teased. She started racing toward the pool. The Flamingoes always gathered there at lunchtime. They waited for the crowd at the snack shack to thin out before they ate.

"Steph, no! Come back!" Anna raced after her.

Stephanie halted as she got close enough to see the Flamingoes. They were gathered around a big table, with their heads bent together.

"What are they doing?" Allie asked when she caught up to Stephanie.

"It looks like they're making decorations or something," Darcy said.

"Yeah, that's definitely what they're doing," Stephanie agreed. "Maybe we should go help them."

"Are you serious? Help the Flamingoes?" Kayla asked.

"Well, I kind of feel sorry for Rene, losing Rick," Stephanie said. "And I hate to say it, but it is our dance, too. We really should help make it look good."

"I guess that's true," Darcy admitted. "I mean, knowing the Flamingoes, all the local news stations will be there to take pictures, anyway."

"You're right." Kayla sighed. "Let's offer to help."

As they approached the Flamingoes, Stephanie began to have second thoughts.

"Maybe I'd better not come with you guys," she muttered. "I really don't want to get into a fight with Rene."

At that moment, Rene glanced up from the pink paper flower she was making. "Stephanie, hi," she called out in her fake-sweet voice. "Come to volunteer? We'll need a couple hundred more of these flowers for the dance."

"Uh, sure, we'll help," Stephanie said. "Show us what you need done."

"No problem. By the way, I think it's really great of you." Rene smiled at Stephanie. "Don't you, Alyssa?"

"I sure do," Alyssa replied.

"Wait a minute," Stephanie said. "Why aren't you acting mad? Didn't you see the latest flyer about the tango lessons?"

"Oh, that!" Rene waved a hand in the air as if to dismiss it. "Even Sandy realized that was a total fake. Besides, don't you know that nothing you do bothers me anymore?"

"It doesn't?" Stephanie asked.

Rene shook her head. "Of course not. All I can think about is going to the dance with the cutest date ever!"

Rene waved across the pool. Stephanie followed Rene's gaze. Her heart did a double flip—Rene was waving to Rick!

Rick pretended not to see.

"Did you tell him to wear a tux?" Alyssa asked.

"Of course. Some of us still want the dance to be formal." Rene sighed happily. "He'll look so adorable. I just can't wait for Saturday night!"

Stephanie stared from Rene to Rick and back to Rene again. She suddenly felt as if she couldn't breathe.

Rick still hadn't broken his date with Rene! Was he really going to do it? Or did he secretly want to go with Rene?

CHAPTER
15

◆ ◀ ◢ ◆

"Ugh, boys!" Stephanie stomped into the living room and flung down her backpack on the nearest chair. "Who needs them?"

D.J. and Michelle glanced up from the television. "Not me!" Michelle said.

"Me neither," Stephanie agreed. She flopped down on the sofa beside Michelle.

"Steph, what happened?" D.J. asked.

"It's Rick!" Stephanie burst out. "He still hasn't broken his date with Rene! I am so mad, I could scream."

"Would you go scream in our room, please? I'm watching this show," Michelle said.

Stephanie ignored her little sister's joke. "I can't believe he lied to me."

The doorbell rang. Michelle jumped up. "I bet that's Cassie," she said. She opened the door. "No, it's not. It's Rick," she called back.

"Is Stephanie here?" Stephanie heard him asking.

"Yes, and she's real mad at you," Michelle answered. "Steph! Rick's here to see you."

Rick appeared in the entrance to the living room. "Hi," he said.

Stephanie refused to look at him.

"Uh, Michelle," D.J. said. "Why don't we go fix ourselves a snack?"

"I'm not hungry," Michelle said.

"Yes, you are," D.J. told her. She grabbed Michelle by the shoulders and steered her into the kitchen.

Rick gave Stephanie an embarrassed grin. "I wanted to talk to you at the pool," he said.

"Then why didn't you?" Stephanie demanded.

"Too many people around," Rick said. He clasped and unclasped his hands, looking uncomfortable. "I know you're mad at me," he went on. "But I just couldn't find the right time to tell Rene I'm not going to the dance with her."

"How hard could it be?" Stephanie asked. "Just say it—I'm not going to the dance with you."

"I will," Rick promised. "And I've tried. Really. I called her last Sunday night, right after we spoke.

114

But she was sleeping over at a friend's house. I tried to get her alone every single day at the pool. But her friends are always hanging around."

"They can't be there every single minute," Stephanie challenged.

"I know you don't believe me," Rick replied. "But I'm telling the truth! Either her friends were hanging around or one of my friends was hanging around." He looked miserable. "I just want to find the right moment, Stephanie."

"What if the right moment doesn't come until Sunday morning?" she asked.

The phone rang, and Stephanie heard D.J. answer in the kitchen. A moment later, she poked her head around the door. "It's Karin's father. He wants to talk to you."

"Tell him I'll call him right back." Stephanie turned to Rick again.

"I know you think I'm stalling again, Steph," Rick said. "But believe me—I said I'd do it, and I will."

Stephanie sighed. She felt awful when Rick wouldn't believe her about the phony letter or about Cody. And she wanted to believe him.

"Okay," she said. "I believe you. But Rick, don't wait too much longer."

*   *   *

"You look fabulous!" Allie's eyes shone as she examined Stephanie's outfit for the dance.

Stephanie turned in front of the mirror in her room to show off the short, flowered sundress. The dress was in shades of deep turquoise and green. She'd added new sandals in the same shade of turquoise. Delicate gold earrings glittered against her cheeks. Her hair was pulled up in front and fell in soft curves over her shoulders.

"You look great, too," Stephanie told Allie.

Allie whirled, modeling her bright yellow skirt and white vest top. She lifted a hand to smooth her hair, and her gold Club Stephanie charm bracelet gleamed.

Kayla had given everyone the delicate bracelets on the night of their first Club Stephanie sleepover.

"Oh! My club bracelet!" Stephanie exclaimed. "Thank goodness I saw yours, Allie. I almost forgot to wear mine!" She fetched it from her jewelry box. Allie helped her fasten it around her wrist.

"Remember when Kayla gave these to us?" Stephanie asked. "It was only two months ago, but it seems like Kayla—and Anna—have been good friends of ours forever."

"I know," Allie agreed. "So much has happened this summer."

Like finding—and losing—the best boyfriend ever, Stephanie added silently.

116

"So did you talk to Rick today?" Allie asked, as if reading her mind.

Stephanie sighed. The daily question had almost become a joke. Every day since Monday, Stephanie had asked Rick if he'd broken the date with Rene. And every day he said no.

"He says he keeps trying," Stephanie explained. "And I keep telling him I believe him."

"He's left it kind of late, hasn't he?" Allie said. "I mean, the dance starts in less than an hour."

"Please, don't remind me," Stephanie said. "If it was anyone but Rick, I would have given up long ago."

"Well, I know I said Rick was worth waiting for," Allie replied. "But this is too much. Maybe it's time to give up, Steph."

"I know you're right," Stephanie said. "It's just really hard to give up on him."

I really thought Rick was someone I could count on, she thought.

She shook her head sadly. "Don't worry, Al, I'm not waiting for Rick anymore. I guess he lied to me about breaking his date." Stephanie blinked back sudden tears that filled her eyes. "But Rick or no Rick, I'm still going to the dance—and I'll dance as hard as I can!"

"That's the spirit," Allie said.

Stephanie forced a smile. "Are we still meeting the others at the pool?"

Allie nodded. "Yeah. And it's time to leave!"

Allie and Stephanie were riding to the pool with Allie's mom, who was waiting outside in the car. Darcy's dad was driving the other girls. D.J., Stephanie's aunt Becky, and her dad planned to drop by later in the evening to cheer them on.

"Wow! Look at this place!" Allie gaped in wonder as Mrs. Taylor pulled into the parking lot.

The community center was totally transformed. All the picnic tables had been carried onto one section of lawn under the trees. Rows and rows of bright lanterns were strung overhead, casting soft shadows over the tables.

The patio itself was cleared for dancing. More lanterns overhead gave it a magical glow.

"It looks fantastic," Stephanie murmured.

"I'm really sorry it didn't work out with Rick," Allie said, giving her a sideways glance.

"It's okay," Stephanie said. "I'll have fun hanging out with you guys. We'll show the world that Club Stephanie can outdance anyone, right?"

"Right," Allie agreed. "Hey, there's Darcy, Kayla, and Anna!" Allie waved, and they hurried to meet the others.

Darcy and Kayla looked great in shiny sleeveless tanks over short, silky skirts.

"But look at Anna!" Stephanie cried.

Anna wore a long, backless dress from a thrift shop. It was dark red satin, with a lighter red feathery pattern all over. Shiny black patent leather sandals gleamed under the hem of the dress. Her arms were bare of her usual stack of bangles.

Her only jewelry was a pair of gleaming silver hoop earrings. They set off the dark gray eyeliner that made her brown eyes look bigger than ever. Her hair curled softly all around her face, showing off her pretty features.

"Anna, you look totally beautiful!" Stephanie exclaimed.

"Thanks. But I don't think it matters too much," Anna said. "There's no chance that Cody will notice me."

"Of course he will," Stephanie told her. "So let's get this dance started."

She led the way onto the patio. Groups of kids were standing around, as if they weren't sure what to do.

"It's weird," Kayla said. "We should hear music by now. The dance was supposed to start at seven, wasn't it?" It was a few minutes past the hour.

"I'm sure they'll start any minute," Allie said.

"Oh, no," Darcy gasped. "What is this?" She bent over a huge plastic sack. It was stuffed with paper flower decorations.

"The Flamingoes didn't bother setting up!" Stephanie exclaimed. "Where are they, anyway?"

She caught sight of Mary Kelly hurrying past. Mary wore a slinky satin dress. Her hair was piled up in little curls on top of her head.

"What happened to the decorations, Mary?" Stephanie called. "Weren't you guys supposed to fix that stuff before anyone got here?"

"Someone else will have to finish," Mary snapped. "We're not getting up on ladders now."

"And look at this!" Anna held out an electrical cord. "No wonder there isn't any music. The speakers aren't rigged up yet!"

"We didn't know how to do that," Mary said. "We thought somebody else could fix it."

"Somebody else who?" Darcy asked. Mary shrugged.

"Well, where are the rest of the Flamingoes?" Stephanie demanded.

"Fixing their hair in the locker room. We'll all be out in a second, okay?" Mary disappeared into the clubhouse.

"Typical," Darcy grunted. "Of course their hair is more important than a sound system that works!"

"What's happening, guys?" Cody appeared. He looked adorable in a pale blue shirt tucked into crisp jeans.

Stephanie saw Anna glance at him and look away.

"Don't ask!" Kayla exclaimed. "The Flamingoes never finished the decorations."

"They didn't even bother setting up the sound system!" Anna added.

"We could hang the decorations ourselves, if we can find a ladder," Darcy said. "But I haven't a clue about speakers."

"I could help," Cody said. "I'm no expert, but I'll give it a try."

He picked up a lead and turned toward a big speaker.

"Wait a second." Anna stopped him. "That lead doesn't hook into a speaker."

"Are you sure?" Cody asked.

"Yup." Anna knelt down beside him. "That's the lead into the mixer." She took the wire from Cody and plugged it into a black unit with knobs and dials on it. "And then this lead goes out to the speakers."

"How do you know about stuff like this?" Cody asked.

"I was stage manager for all our school plays," Anna replied. "I always helped rig up the sound system."

"Cool," Cody said. "So where do you think we should put this speaker?"

Allie poked Stephanie, and they both grinned. Finally Anna and Cody were getting along!

Stephanie helped Darcy set up a ladder, and soon the patio was full of flowers draped near the lanterns overhead. The flowers looked real in the lantern light.

As Stephanie climbed down the ladder, she saw Anna sneaking out of the girls' locker room.

I wonder what she was doing in there? Stephanie wondered. A moment later, Anna whispered something to Cody. They both laughed.

Suddenly a burst of sound blasted out of the speakers. Cody and Anna leaped up and slapped each other high fives.

"This girl is incredible," Cody declared as he and Anna hurried over to the others. "You should have seen how quickly she got that system rigged up. She's coming over to hook up my new stereo tomorrow."

Anna smiled shyly.

"That's great," Stephanie said. "But I don't hear any music."

"Yeah. Isn't it working now?" Darcy asked.

"Sure," Anna said. "We just need to test this microphone."

She turned a knob on the mixer.

"Hurry up, you guys!" A girl's high voice

boomed across the patio. "We should get out there! We can't let the dance start without us."

"Plus there's tons of stuff we haven't done yet," a second voice replied.

Stephanie stared at Anna in surprise. "That sounds like Mary and Alyssa," she said.

"Oh, who cares about the stupid dance, anyway?" a third voice chimed in.

The third voice was definitely Rene's!

Stephanie stared at Anna in amazement. "The Flamingoes are in the locker room," she said. "And you're broadcasting every word they're saying!"

CHAPTER
16

◆ ◢ ◣ ◆

Stephanie stared at Anna, openmouthed. "Did you rig it up like that on purpose?" she asked.

Anna giggled. "Pretty wild, huh? And they have no idea anybody can hear them!"

"I'm already bored with the whole dance-a-thon," Rene's voice rang out. "I wish I'd never agreed to be chairperson. This whole fund-raising thing is stupid."

"But what about saving the pool?" Alyssa asked.

Rene laughed. "I don't care if they save the crummy pool or not," she said. "We'll all be back at the country club next summer. They'll be finished fixing it up then—and the country club pool is tons nicer than this dump. In fact, they could pull down this place tomorrow and it wouldn't bother me."

"But Rene, you made us work so hard getting pledges!" Cynthia protested.

"I know. But we had to do it. We had to show up those Club Stephanie geeks," Rene said.

"I agree with Rene," Darah's voice chimed in. "This place *is* a dump."

"And the kids here are lame, too," Tiffany added.

"Total losers, all of them," Rene declared. "But I suppose we'll have to get out there and pretend that we're having fun. After all, that TV reporter is supposed to interview me again. And I love being on TV."

Rene and the Flamingoes appeared in the doorway. They all wore long, fancy dresses like Mary's. Rene's was bright pink.

Someone booed and hooted at them. Suddenly everyone at the dance was hissing and jeering.

Rene's mouth dropped open in astonishment. The other Flamingoes looked as surprised as she did.

"What's going on here?" Rene demanded.

"Oh, nothing much," Stephanie told her. "It's just that no one was very happy to know that you think we're all a bunch of losers."

"What? When did I ever say that?" Rene asked, acting totally innocent.

"Just now in the locker room. We heard every word," Darcy told her.

"You what?" Rene looked horrified.

"Your entire conversation got picked up on one of the mikes," Allie added.

Rene spun around to Stephanie. "Is this your idea of a joke?"

"Not really," Stephanie said. "There's nothing funny about the way you just put down everyone here. But I'm glad we all got to hear what you really think about saving the pool."

"Yeah—" someone called across the patio. "And we don't care if you and your pink friends never come back, either!"

"Flamingoes stink!" someone else yelled. "Pink stinks!"

In an instant, everyone was shouting and stamping their feet: "Pink stinks! Pink stinks!"

Stephanie grinned at her friends. Allie slapped her a high five.

"At last!" Darcy crowed. "We get our revenge!"

"You're right!" Stephanie exclaimed in surprise. "This is the best revenge—finally everyone knows how awful the Flamingoes really are!"

"Oh, who cares what you think?" Rene tossed her head. "Look," she said, pointing across the patio. Stephanie saw a newspaper photographer arriving. The camera crew from the local TV station that had interviewed Rene at the mall was right behind him.

"That's all I care about," Rene said. "Because the Flamingoes deserve the credit for saving this pool. And I'll make sure we get it. See you after my interview!" She waved and hurried toward the reporters.

"Attention, everyone!" Sandy stood near the snack shack, speaking into a microphone. "It's time for the dance-a-thon to begin. Will everyone find your partners, please?"

Stephanie felt her heart sink. It was the moment she'd been dreading. *How will I ever stand watching Rene dance with Rick all night?* she wondered.

"Stephanie! Over here!"

Stephanie was surprised to see Rick striding across the patio. He looked cuter than ever in a tan linen jacket over a white T-shirt and black pants.

"Hi," he said as he reached her side.

Stephanie felt a burst of annoyance. "Hi, yourself," she answered.

"So, do you have a date for tonight?" Rick asked with a grin.

"Huh? Why, what do you mean?" Stephanie gazed at him in confusion.

Rick laughed. "What I mean is, will you be my date?"

"Your date?" Stephanie repeated. "But what happened? I thought you never broke your date with Rene."

"I didn't—until this afternoon," Rick said. "I knew you didn't believe that I was really trying to do it. Then I finally realized what was going on."

"I don't understand," Stephanie told him.

"Rene was avoiding me on purpose," Rick said. "She even admitted it. She saw us together the day we made up. She guessed that I wanted to break my date with her. So she made herself impossible to track down. That's why she never answered my calls. And she made sure I couldn't talk to her at the pool, either."

"I should have guessed," Stephanie murmured.

Rick laughed. "I was getting pretty desperate," he said. "But I figured that she had to go home before the dance tonight to get dressed. So I camped out on her doorstep to make sure I was there when she showed."

"Oh, Rick!" Stephanie laughed. "I bet she wasn't too happy to see you."

"She didn't take it too well," Rick admitted.

"You're probably on her worst-enemies list now," Stephanie said. "Right after me."

"As long as I'm with you, I don't care," Rick

answered. He reached for both her hands and held them tight.

Music played, and Rick and Stephanie began to dance. Stephanie was thrilled to see Cody lead Anna to the dance floor. Darcy was nearby, dancing with Billy Golden. Kayla and Jack Kramer danced past. Allie and Mike the lifeguard spun near them. They made a great team.

The music was upbeat and bouncy, and everyone looked as if they were having the time of their lives. Stephanie noticed that Rene had grabbed Timothy Borden for a partner. Timothy was a ninth-grader and often hung out with the Flamingoes. He wasn't much of a dancer, though. Stephanie heard Rene give a sudden yelp of pain.

"You stepped on my foot, you klutz," she yelled at Timothy. "I think it's broken!" Rene limped off the floor. "I'll lose pledges, thanks to you!" she fumed.

"It's too bad for the pool," Rick said to Stephanie.

"Yeah—and now Rene won't even get her picture in the paper or on TV," Stephanie added. "Rene looks so upset, I almost feel sorry for her."

"Don't," Rick said. "She deserved it. And this crowd is really into dancing. I bet we make up for her lost pledges."

Everyone danced as if they would never get

tired. Still, as the hours passed, the music changed. There were more slow dances, and Stephanie was glad. She had never danced for such a long time before. But she barely felt tired. She felt as if she could dance forever, as long as she danced with Rick!

Sandy moved among the dancing couples. Some of them were so tired, they were barely moving. They leaned against each other, shuffling their feet from side to side. If they were doing more leaning than dancing, Sandy tapped their shoulders, and they were out of the dance-a-thon.

Each time a couple left the dance floor, the crowd of people watching clapped and cheered.

Another slow dance began to play. Then another. And another. Anna and Cody gave up. Then Allie and Mike were out of the dance-a-thon.

Soon it was almost eleven o'clock. Stephanie and Rick had been dancing for almost four hours straight! Only three other couples were dancing. They were all Flamingoes.

I'm not letting one of them beat me, Stephanie thought. *I can dance as long as they can!*

Stephanie could feel her dress sticking to her back. Her legs felt as if they were made of lead. She tried not to groan out loud.

"I never thought dancing could be so hard," Rick murmured.

"Tell me about it," Stephanie replied. "But we can't quit yet. One more hour means a few hundred dollars more for the pool."

"I know." Rick straightened his shoulders. "We won't stop."

Finally only Stephanie and Rick were left dancing. Everyone else watched from the edge of the patio. Sandy raced onto the dance floor, her arms raised high in the air.

"It's midnight," she announced. "This dance-a-thon is officially over!"

Stephanie and Rick stared at each other in delight. "We did it!" Stephanie collapsed against his shoulder.

"We made a great team," Rick told her, giving her a big hug.

"We sure did," Stephanie agreed.

Darcy, Allie, and Kayla rushed onto the patio. Anna and Cody followed them. So did Stephanie's father and D.J.

"You guys were great!" Danny exclaimed, beaming at Stephanie in pride.

"I got tired just watching you," D.J. admitted.

Sandy called for attention. "First of all, I want to tell our dancers—you did a terrific job!"

Everyone clapped and shouted and whistled. Then Sandy began to read out the amounts each dancer had earned. Stephanie had mixed feelings as she listened. She was thrilled at how much money the pledges had brought in. But it was clear that the Flamingoes had raised more money than Club Stephanie—even without Rene.

"I guess we should just be happy that we tried to keep the pool open," Stephanie replied.

"Stephanie Tanner and Rick Summers," Sandy called out. "Tally, three hundred and twenty dollars!"

"Hold on! I'd like to add to that amount," a deep voice called.

"Mr. Carver!" Stephanie gaped in surprise as Karin's father appeared at the edge of the patio. He pushed his way through the crowd and stepped up to her.

Oops—I never called him back! she suddenly remembered.

"Mr. Carver, I'm sorry," Stephanie called to him. "I was supposed to call you back and—"

"It's okay," Mr. Carver said, smiling. "I figured you were busy. So I thought I'd bring my pledge down here myself. I hope I'm not too late."

"Of course you're not," Sandy said. "Any little bit helps."

"Then please accept this." Mr. Carver handed Sandy a check.

She looked at it, and her mouth dropped open. "But . . . but this is for ten thousand dollars!"

132

Mr. Carver nodded. "That's right. I admire hard work, and Stephanie and her friends have shown they're willing to work hard—for something that means a lot to them."

"I don't know how to thank you," Sandy said.

"My thanks is that I'll help keep this community center open," Mr. Carver replied. "And if that check isn't enough, I'll make sure you get more, from all my business associates." He paused and motioned Stephanie closer. "Besides, I owe you a special favor, Stephanie. I can never repay you for what you've done for my daughter."

The reporters rushed up, snapping pictures and calling questions to Stephanie. She answered as fast as she could.

"Well, congratulations, everyone," Sandy finally said. "It looks like the pool *will* stay open, thanks to all of you!"

The whole crowd burst into more cheers and applause. Rene stomped up to Stephanie. The rest of the Flamingoes trailed behind her.

"Well, you win, Stephanie," she said. "This is the last time you'll see the Flamingoes at your crummy pool!" Rene grabbed Alyssa's arm. The Flamingoes stormed out of the community center.

Stephanie glanced up at Rick. "You're not sorry, Rick, are you?" she asked. "I mean, not everyone was against the Flamingoes this summer. And I know you liked Rene at first, and—"

Rick cut her off. "I don't think anyone here will miss the Flamingoes," he said. He grinned, and Stephanie smiled back at him.

Darcy raced up to Stephanie. "You know what this means, don't you?" she asked. "It means we'll all be back next summer!"

"I can't wait," Rick told her.

Kayla, Anna, Stephanie, Allie, and Darcy threw their arms around each other.

The photographer stepped forward and snapped their picture. "Great story," he said. "And this is a great shot. I bet it will make the front page!"

"And I have the perfect caption," Stephanie told him. "Just title it, Club Stephanie Rules—Forever!"

FULL HOUSE™
Stephanie

PHONE CALL FROM A FLAMINGO	88004-7/$3.99
THE BOY-OH-BOY NEXT DOOR	88121-3/$3.99
TWIN TROUBLES	88290-2/$3.99
HIP HOP TILL YOU DROP	88291-0/$3.99
HERE COMES THE BRAND NEW ME	89858-2/$3.99
THE SECRET'S OUT	89859-0/$3.99
DADDY'S NOT-SO-LITTLE GIRL	89860-4/$3.99
P.S. FRIENDS FOREVER	89861-2/$3.99
GETTING EVEN WITH THE FLAMINGOES	52273-6/$3.99
THE DUDE OF MY DREAMS	52274-4/$3.99
BACK-TO-SCHOOL COOL	52275-2/$3.99
PICTURE ME FAMOUS	52276-0/$3.99
TWO-FOR-ONE CHRISTMAS FUN	53546-3/$3.99
THE BIG FIX-UP MIX-UP	53547-1/$3.99
TEN WAYS TO WRECK A DATE	53548-X/$3.99
WISH UPON A VCR	53549-8/$3.99
DOUBLES OR NOTHING	56841-8/$3.99
SUGAR AND SPICE ADVICE	56842-6/$3.99
NEVER TRUST A FLAMINGO	56843-4/$3.99
THE TRUTH ABOUT BOYS	00361-5/$3.99
CRAZY ABOUT THE FUTURE	00362-3/$3.99

Available from Minstrel® Books Published by Pocket Books

FULL HOUSE™
Club Stephanie

Summer is here and Stephanie is ready for some fun!

A brand-new miniseries! Collect all three books.

#1 Fun, Sun, and Flamingoes
#2 Fireworks and Flamingoes
#3 Flamingo Revenge

-All Now Available-

Based on the hit Warner Bros. TV series!

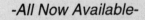

A MINSTREL® BOOK
Published by Pocket Books

1357-01

FULL HOUSE™
Michelle

#1: THE GREAT PET PROJECT 51905-0/$3.50

#2: THE SUPER-DUPER SLEEPOVER PARTY
51906-9/$3.50

#3: MY TWO BEST FRIENDS 52271-X/$3.99

#4: LUCKY, LUCKY DAY 52272-8/$3.50

#5: THE GHOST IN MY CLOSET 53573-0/$3.99

#6: BALLET SURPRISE 53574-9/$3.99

#7: MAJOR LEAGUE TROUBLE 53575-7/$3.99

#8: MY FOURTH-GRADE MESS 53576-5/$3.99

#9: BUNK 3, TEDDY, AND ME 56834-5/$3.99

#10: MY BEST FRIEND IS A MOVIE STAR!
(Super Edition) 56835-3/$3.99

#11: THE BIG TURKEY ESCAPE 56836-1/$3.99

#12: THE SUBSTITUTE TEACHER 00364-X/$3.99

#13: CALLING ALL PLANETS 00365-8/$3.50

#14: I'VE GOT A SECRET 00366-6/$3.99

#15: HOW TO BE COOL 00833-1/$3.99

A MINSTREL® BOOK

Published by Pocket Books

Simon & Schuster Mail Order Dept. BWB
200 Old Tappan Rd., Old Tappan, N.J. 07675

Please send me the books I have checked above. I am enclosing $_____(please add $0.75 to cover the postage and handling for each order. Please add appropriate sales tax). Send check or money order--no cash or C.O.D.'s please. Allow up to six weeks for delivery. For purchase over $10.00 you may use VISA: card number, expiration date and customer signature must be included.

Name _____

Address _____

City _____ State/Zip _____

VISA Card # _____ Exp.Date _____

Signature _____

1033-19

It doesn't matter if you live around the corner...
or around the world...
If you are a fan of Mary-Kate and Ashley Olsen,
you should be a member of

MARY-KATE + ASHLEY'S FUN CLUB™

Here's what you get:
Our Funzine™
An autographed color photo
Two black & white individual photos
A full size color poster
An official **Fun Club**™ membership card
A **Fun Club**™ school folder
Two special **Fun Club**™ surprises
A holiday card
Fun Club™ collectibles catalog
Plus a **Fun Club**™ box to keep everything in

To join Mary-Kate + Ashley's Fun Club™, fill out the form
below and send it along with

U.S. Residents – $17.00
Canadian Residents – $22 U.S. Funds
International Residents – $27 U.S. Funds

MARY-KATE + ASHLEY'S FUN CLUB™
859 HOLLYWOOD WAY, SUITE 275
BURBANK, CA 91505

NAME:_____

ADDRESS:_____

_CITY:_____ STATE:_____ ZIP:_____

PHONE:(____) _____ BIRTHDATE:_____

1242